PALE
WINTER SUN

Roses are red
Violets are blue
Pickles are green
I'm not a poet

This is a work of fiction. Names, characters, business, etc, etc, are used in fictitious manner and resemblances to actual persons, living, dead, or otherwise is purely coincidental and kinda weird. Grason and Cache are completely made up towns and we're still trying to figure out if Idaho is real or not.

For Sierra

I.

On Tuesday, Hannah Robinson was caught in a heavy make-out session with her best friend Lindsey Smith. Hannah's brother, Mitchell, took credit with the discovery by walking into her room without knocking. His sibling disregard for her personal space yet again disrupted her plans. On Wednesday, she had been forbidden to leave her house. On Thursday, Lindsey had been taken out of school. On Saturday night, Mark Jensen sat in an abandoned house, lit by a full September moon shining through a naked window. Across from him floated a pinprick of orange light in the dark.

"I guess Lindsey is on suicide watch," Mark said. "They won't let her get near Hannah. She may be a cutter, but I doubt this is enough to kill herself over."

"Mitchell told me that Hannah finally admitted to her parents that she is a lesbian," a voice said behind the lit cigarette. Trevor Buell leaned forward into the light, his face a mass of smoke and shadows. "When she told them that Lindsey was her girlfriend, they flipped out. Bishop Johns has spent the entire week going between Lindsey's house and Hannah's house."

"Why did they have to get caught?" Mark anguished. "Church tomorrow is going to suck. It's going to be all about 'coming together' and 'call upon each other to help them in their time of need.'"

"I'm sure coming together is something those two don't need help with." Trevor said as he offered his cigarette. Mark waved it away.

"My mom will give me crap for smelling like smoke as it is. I don't need it on my breath." He put his head back. The sound of it hitting the wall echoed in the empty house. "You know what this means?"

"Witch hunt," Trevor answered. "It'll be like when they found Jeordie Ward's older sister smoking weed behind the seminary. They'll shake us all down, ask us a million questions, but this time check our phones for pictures of dicks instead of our pockets for drugs." Mark heard the chains of Trevor's biker jacket jingle. No one was more amused at Trevor's little jokes than Trevor.

"Speaking of Jeordie," Trevor continued, "you two better watch out. They'll be checking your breath for penis."

"We haven't gone that far," Mark said, glad the night hid the reddening of his cheeks. "Besides, it's not like we're dating; we're just…hanging out." He stood up; he didn't like talking to Trevor about his non-relationship with Jeordie. He always had something mean to say about it. "Let's go. If my mom catches us in one of her empty houses again, she'll kill me. And don't put that out in here." Trevor grunted and followed him out. Mark often took advantage of his mother's job in real estate, but he rarely did anything more than sit and watch Trevor smoke.

As soon as they stepped outside he flicked the butt into the overgrown back yard. An unseasonable cold front had settled on southern Idaho and northern Utah. The fall leaves were crisper than usual as they crunched underneath the teenage boys' feet. Their jackets were open, though, despite the chill that nipped at their nose and face. The two fifteen-year-olds walked casually with one another. They were an exercise in differences. Both of them had dark hair that danced in the breeze, but the similarities ended there. The taller of the two wore a black and white Adidas track suit with an army-style jacket over it. His deep eyes occasionally darted around, as if searching for something to search for. The other boy wore a scuffed and worn leather biker jacket. His shaggy hair hung down, hiding his piercing blue eyes but not the permanent grin that always seem to inhabit the corners of his mouth.

"I don't know what you see in him. He's about as smart as a box of rocks and not that cute," Trevor complained.

"He's nice. And he's good looking in a…I don't know…"

"'We're stuck in Idaho' sort of way," Trevor finished for him. Mark gave him a shove as they emerged onto the street. As the teenagers walked towards their respective homes, they could feel the temperature drop further so they hugged their jackets tighter, unprepared for the coming winter.

When Mark entered the warmth of his house, he was immediately greeted by the sight of his father sitting in front of the news and his mother finishing up dinner. The house was a cozy three bedroom that his parents bought right after his older brother Isaac was born. Four years later, Mark came along, and they talked about getting something bigger for their growing family. They continued to talk about it until it became apparent that their family might not be growing anymore. For his parents' deep Mormon beliefs, this caused years of prayers and consternation. Up until six months ago, that is, when his mom came home from the doctor's office, completely beside herself with happiness. She was finally pregnant again. Since his brother Isaac left for college, the house felt empty. Tonight it felt stifling.

"You just missed Isaac's call. He wanted to talk to you." His mother wiped a crumb off of the counter and leaned against it, her pregnant belly weighing on her.

"I'll talk to him next time," Mark said quietly and tried to slip past her. Her sense of smell had become stronger in the last couple months, and he wanted to get Trevor's smoke scent off before she picked up on it.

"You haven't talked to him once since he left for Brigham Young University. I know he has called your cell phone." Mark just shrugged his shoulders in reply and continued inching down the hallway to his room. Even with Isaac off to school, he felt under his shadow. "Where were you, by the way?"

"Just out with Trevor," he said then regretted it, knowing where the conversation was heading.

"I'm not sure I want you hanging out with him so much. Sandy, his mother, says he comes home smelling like smoke, and…well…with what happen to Lindsey…" She struggled for the words as he took another step backwards.

"Sometimes when he talks, he sounds a little light in the loafers," his father finished for her.

"LaVell!" she chided him

"It's the truth. I'm not saying he is, but I haven't seen him with any girls either," he continued, not even looking away from the television. Mark could see the top of his head, thinning hair desperately doing its best to hang on.

"I don't have a girlfriend. Does that make me 'light in the loafers'? Would you rather I knock some girl up now, at fifteen?" Anger was rising in Mark, and he was doing a poor job at containing it. He had been unduly tense lately. Since Lindsey and Hannah had been caught, he felt smothered in his own skin. He hated having to hide who he was to his own family, but he couldn't see any scenario where coming out could possibly go well for him.

"Of course not," she said quickly. "I just worry, that's all. There are a lot of negative influences out there. This life is full of trials and sometimes it can be hard to make the right decisions." Mark gritted his teeth, sensing another one of his mother's dining table sermons.

"Mark, clean up and then set the table for dinner," LaVell said, standing from his chair and shutting off the television. Grateful for the respite, Mark quickly did as he was told.

After dinner, Mark lounged in his room, reading. His room was a typical teenager's room: some clothes that hadn't made it to the hamper yet, books and video game covers scattered about, and posters on the wall. He had adorned the walls with a number of pictures of gorgeous super novae and space shuttles. He turned the page on the book he was reading: *Dahlgren*, by Samuel Delany.

It wasn't a difficult book to read, but it had been slow going. The story of a post-apocalyptic city in a non-post-apocalyptic world wasn't the problem. An immense world of freedom resided in the pages, a freedom he yearned for, with little accountability for its main character. But there was also a sense of madness, of danger that lurked in the chaos that Mark wasn't so sure about. He wanted freedom, he wanted a little chaos, but he remained afraid of the danger and of the price. Grason, Idaho seemed too small for him, but it wasn't the town, it was the people. Some days it felt like the entire population of fifty thousand suffocated him. He wasn't just hiding behind a bedroom door or behind a book; he was hiding inside his own skin. Every day and in front of almost everybody he pretended not to be gay and pretended that he wasn't going against the church's teachings. His family wouldn't understand. They were Latter Day Saints and Idaho bred. Grason wasn't some tiny hick town, but it wasn't far off, and bigger ideas sometimes took a while to settle in.

Few people knew his secret. Trevor and Jeordie obviously knew, as well as a couple of his classmates. None of his family knew, but he often wondered if his brother Isaac suspected. He never said anything outright, but Mark always got the feeling he knew something. It didn't matter much as far as Mark was concerned. Isaac held rank as the Golden Boy in Mark's mind. He was the football and basketball player, got fantastic grades, and everybody loved him. But he wasn't here anymore. He had gone off to college. Despite it all, Mark carried a sense of abandonment since his brother left to college. This abandonment slowly turned to resentment, but it wasn't personal; it fed a bigger discontentment. It felt as if he crawled around in his own skin, suffocating and struggling while he died incrementally every day.

Attempting to use reading in order to escape this scatter-shot mix of uncertainty didn't help as much as he'd hoped. The main character of the story lived between lapses of time, and in those lapses he found himself between the beds of both a man and a woman. Something deep within Mark shifted and tried to come to the surface. He wanted to swallow it down, but it got harder each time. The ease in which the transitions between loving man and woman occurred left him uncomfortable as he read on. If gay is a one-way street, he wondered, why am I always wanting to look both ways?

II.

Mid-afternoon on Sunday found Mark and Trevor standing on the front lawn of the church, looking uncomfortable in their shirts and ties.

"Jesus, they laid it on thick today," Trevor quietly commented. "It felt like Bishop Johns was talking to me the whole time with his 'it's not the Heavenly Father's way but we can help these lost people.' I almost started laughing. 'Let us not cast them out but cast out the sin instead.' It's going to take more than prayer to straighten me out."

"Yeah," Mark mumbled, too busy scanning the emerging church goers.

"Jeordie is helping teach Sunday School. He'll be out in a minute. Jeez, you're single-minded lately." Trevor rolled his eyes and scoffed. "There's my dad. I'm out. I'll talk to you later." As he walked off, Mark finally caught sight of his target. The tall, round-faced teenager was talking and shaking hands with an Elder. Casually, Mark made his way to them.

"Hey. Some sermon, huh?" Mark tried to say knowingly. Jeordie took the hint but wasn't comfortable about it.

"Gives a lot to think about, I guess," he replied. The two of them ran out of words and stood there awkwardly for a moment. Mark's father walked up and broke the silence.

"Time to go." The boys said their goodbyes as Mark followed his parents to the car. Jeordie watched Mark go then turned to face the building of God. Though Mark was preoccupied with his thoughts about his crush, the sermon wasn't totally lost on him. It certainly wasn't lost on his mother. Car rides from church had the same pattern; his father drove in quiet contemplation while his mother talked in short bursts. Sometimes about the sermon, other times about what activities she was going to participate in, but today it was all about "poor Lindsey" and "that Hannah."

"That Hannah has always been a handful. I know that she has her trials to go through, like all of us, but I can't believe she tried to bring poor Lindsey down with her," she prattled on. Mark tried to ignore her, the conversation making him antsy and uncomfortable. Isaac handled these rides home the best because he knew how to distract her and get her off topic. Mark's favorite was the horribly awkward masturbation rant that somehow his brother managed to smoothly

11

transition to the best potato salad recipe. Mark lacked such finesse. The best he felt he could do was say as little as possible so he didn't encourage more discussion.

"She has a hard road ahead of her," LaVell said as he tailgated the rusty truck in front of him. His driving was never worse than on Sunday afternoons.

They pulled up to their house to find Clara's sister Caryn waiting for them. Mark saw some hope for the day yet; he liked his Aunt Caryn. She came off more down to earth than his parents and seemed to be more understanding and less dogmatic.

"I love her sports car," LaVell said they pulled into the driveway.

"I don't know if a Miata is considered a sports car," Mark said.

"Regardless, I'm glad she got it. When your Uncle Steve died, she needed something to lift her spirits, and that little car seems to do it," LaVell said while Clara sighed. Even though Caryn was at church almost as much as her sister, Mark always got the feeling that she wished that Aunt Caryn would have put more faith in God at the passing of her husband and less faith in the little red Mazda.

Once inside, the sisters landed in the living room to talk amongst themselves, mainly about Clara's pregnancy and Isaac being gone. LaVell shrugged off his suit and plopped in his chair, looking for a game on the television. Mark disappeared into his room and tossed the brown leather Book of Mormon on his desk, where it landed with a solid thud. He fell across his bed, remembering an essay for tomorrow's English class, but he knew he couldn't focus. The small smoldering inside of him, left over from their short conversation in the car, wouldn't let him. There was always blame and Jesus with his parents. For every action there had to be someone at fault, and the only path out was to get right with God.

"But what if no one is to blame? What if there is nothing wrong?" he asked out loud. With no answer forthcoming, he got up and wandered into the kitchen in search of something to drink.

"Don't spoil your dinner," LaVell called out preemptively. Mark rolled his eyes and opened the refrigerator.

"She has a hard road ahead of her," Caryn said, echoing Clara's words from earlier. Mark could only guess they were talking about the reason for today's sermon again.

"That she does," Clara agreed with gusto. "She is going to have to get right with The Heavenly Father and pray that she didn't drag poor Lindsey too far down that path with her."

Against his better judgment, Mark blurted out, "Has anyone considered that maybe Lindsey wanted to make out with her? And so what if they did? They just kissed. It wasn't like they found her with her head buried deep in her…"

"Hey!" his father interrupted. "Watch your tongue."

"Two fifteen year old girls don't need to be kissing each other. Same as two fifteen year old boys. There are set rules against it that came from above, and the less we mind them, the worse the world becomes," Clara said to Mark then took a deep breath. "Someone is inside just kicking up a storm. Baby Rachel is active today."

As Mark poured a tall glass of milk, the women cooed over his mother's stomach until Caryn said, "You know, I think this thing with those two girls has

14

been a little overblown. They're just kids." Mark stopped mid gulp.

"That's exactly the point," his father added. "They don't know better, and they need shepherded back on the right path."

"Yeah, but is it so bad?" Caryn continued. Mark wished she would both carry on *and* stop. As much effort as he took to hide the real him from his parents, there were times he just wanted to scream it in their faces. Just run a giant gay pride parade through the living room with him as the grand marshal. He didn't have the guts and he knew it. He appreciated his aunt for her more open-minded view, but he was afraid that she could also somehow blow his cover in the process.

"It's a sin, plain and simple. People try and complicate the issue to justify it, but it's the scriptures. You can't get more direct than that," Clara pontificated.

Deciding that he'd had enough of this conversation, Mark shuffled off to his room. Just as he passed the living room, Caryn asked, "What if Mark came to you and said he was gay?" Mark stopped dead and looked at his aunt. She looked up at him briefly and their eyes met. A jolt ran through him, mind and body, as he realized that she knew. He had been found out.

Clara scoffed. "Mark isn't that way. He's on the right path. Both of my boys are." Before Caryn could look up again, Mark made a point to disappear back into his room.

Later, Mark bent over his laptop watching the cursor blink on a blank white screen. No matter how hard he tried, he couldn't seem to find anything to say about Thoreau. His stomach heard the sounds of dinner being prepared and responded accordingly. There was a knock at his door.

"Hey, kiddo," Aunt Caryn said as she came in. "How's it going?"

"Fine. I just have a case of writer's block on this essay," Mark said, grateful for the distraction.

His aunt sat on the bed, her dress a bit more fashionable in contrast to his mother's usual dour Sunday attire."Must be strange not having your brother around," she said, easing into the conversation. "Soon you'll have a little sister, though."

"Yeah. That'll be cool, I guess," They lapsed into a thick silence before he asked, "So how long have you known?"

"I've suspected it for a while," she admitted.

"Oh," was all he could think to say. His spirit rose, but only so far as it still remained tethered by fear. "Are you going to tell my parents?"

"No. That's not up to me. I would prefer that you weren't this way, but you are, and I still love you."

"Thanks," he said. She stood and gave him a hug.

"These are tough years for you and being this way can only make it tougher. If you need anything, even just to talk, you can always call on me."

She left him to his essay, but he fell upon his bed instead. A warm sensation settled in his chest. He enjoyed it for a moment but realized he couldn't trust it. It felt good to have an ally, to share his secret, but the fear still lingered.

He tried again to work on his essay and got two paragraphs in when his phone buzzed with a text message from Jeordie.

Wanted to hang with you after church but the family had other plans, it read.

Mine too. No worries. Maybe after soccer practice tomorrow? Mark texted back.

After a moment the reply came back: *Sure.* Then, *Send me a dick pic.* Mark thought about it for a moment then typed, *Can't, I'm playing hard to get. :)* There was excitement in the attention, but he felt that there couldn't be enough caution right now. His phone vibrated one more time. This time it was Trevor.

I scored a couple beers and broke past the parental controls on the internet. Let's get weird.

He typed back *Not tonight. My parents are busting out the torches and sharpening the pitchforks, so I better play it safe.*

Party pooper, was the reply.

III.

"I hate soccer practice," Trevor said, adjusting the collar of his leather coat.

The chill wind came off the white tipped mountains that sat on the far horizon. The flat brown farmland and empty sage brush dotted terrain that spread out between Grason and the mountains did little to impede it.

"Then why are you coming with me?" Mark asked. "You're not even on the team. Coach hates it when you sit and watch."

It was the only sport that Mark participated in. At first, he only joined the team to keep his dad off his back. Isaac had been the all-star football player and point guard, depending on which sporting season it was. Despite Mark's normal bookishness, he had to admit he did enjoy it more than he thought he would.

"I've got nothing better to do. My parents redid the child lock on the internet, and there's nothing good on TV. Besides, I like watching you guys run up and down the field in your shorts." Trevor nudged him with his elbow. "Getting under ol' Coach Ward's skin is fun too."

"You do realize that when you piss him off, he takes it out on me, right?" Mark asked him rhetorically. Trevor didn't care about such things because dealing with consequences wasn't his style. Mark had come to peace with it years ago. Mark, the more reserved, let Trevor act the fool and provide the entertainment for them both. It was one of the bonds they shared.

"I suppose Jeordie will be there as well," Trevor noted, barely hiding his contempt

"He's on the team, so yeah, he'll be there," Mark said defensively. They reached the slowly dying grass of the sprawling soccer field. The team was already sprinting and bouncing white and black balls as they warmed up. Mark ran ahead as Trevor moseyed his way to the bleachers. The only other spectators were a couple of girls, obviously there to watch their boyfriends.

"Nice of you to join us, Jensen. can we get started now?" Coach Ward barked.

Mark said a hurried apology as he threw his coat half-heartedly toward Trevor and sprinted out to the field. The soccer coach gave the shaggy teen a quick contemptuous glance before turning his attention to the team.

Ninety minutes later, all the boys came walking back towards the bleachers. They were hot and sweaty, tired and tight from chasing each other up and down the field. Trevor climbed down and handed Mark his coat.

"You ready?" Trevor asked.

"I'm going to hang here for a little bit," Mark told him, paying more attention to Jeordie but talking to Trevor. Trevor just rolled his eyes and walked off.

Mark and Jeordie sat on the grass next to each other, facing away from the setting sun.

"Coach tried to run us to death today," Jeordie said, wiping the last of the cooled sweat off his brow.

"I really think he wants to win state this year. I think we might have a chance," Mark said. "We could beat Idaho Falls this time."

"With you on the team we do. You have quick feet." Jeordie picked at the grass between his legs.

"Thanks, you too." Mark tried not to blush.

They lapsed into nervous silence. The air was beginning to carry a heavier chill, but neither one had any inclination of moving.

"Are you ready for the math test on Friday? I am going to fail it so hard. I just do not get it." Jeordie said, trying to fill in the silence.

"We can get together tomorrow and study if you want," Mark offered.

"Yeah. We can go study at my house. You're the math whiz who wants to go into space and work for NASA," Jeordie said quickly.

"I don't know about going into space. My goal is to work at NASA, though, as an engineer."

"You mean building space shuttles and satellites?"

"Exactly. Have you ever seen the Cassini photos from Saturn? They're gorgeous. It looks as if a professional photographer had gone up there carefully taking each shot from orbit. Or the mountains of data we're getting back from Mars, or the Sun even. It would be a dream come true to be a part of that. To build the machines that brought us all that wonder," Mark said, impassioned. He blushed at Jeordie watching him raptly as he talked.

"I like that about you. You have this dream that you are so excited about. You know exactly what you want, and you have the skills to get there. I can't math to save my ass, but you're like a whiz at it." Jeordie shook his head, "I have no idea what I want. My dad has me help at my uncle's farm all the time, and I think they want me to take it over once I get out of college."

"Nothing wrong with farming. We need farms and cute farmers." Mark said. Jeordie stared at the grass again, but there was a huge smile on his face.

"I don't mind it, I guess. But a space engineer sounds so much more glamorous."

"Hardly." Mark abruptly changed the subject. "You know I like you right?" It was no secret to them both their feelings for each other, Mark knew that, but they had never actually talked about it.

"Yeah. And I like you too." Jeordie said quietly. Unconsciously he looked around the empty field, looking for eavesdroppers.

"Maybe we can do something together, you know, as two people who like each other."

"Like a date?"

"Yeah. We could go catch a movie or something. All we ever do is text each other." Mark said. "I would love to spend more time with you."

Jeordie was quiet for a moment before carefully saying, "I would like that too, but it's just that I...we have to be careful. I mean, if people found out that we were gay…they wouldn't understand."

23

"No, I get it. Trust me, the last thing I want is for my parents to find out. They would have a nuclear meltdown. Ever since my mom got pregnant, she's been on a 'law of the Bible' kick. But there is nothing saying two friends can't go to a movie. Trevor and I do it all the time," Mark said.

"Yeah." Jeordie scowled at the mention of Mark's best friend. "For the longest time I thought that you were with him. Well, until I saw him kissing some college guy last summer."

Mark shook his head and suppressed a smile. Trevor's exploits with Elder Gorrell last summer provided him with more than a little entertainment. For only being a freshman, Trevor did his best to corrupt the soon-to-be missionary before his send-off to some godless land. "You're probably not the first to wonder that. We've been friends for as long as I can remember. But always just that, nothing more. It would seem too weird to think of him any other way."

"You're both queer and have known each other for that long, but nothing ever happened between you two?" Jeordie gave him a skeptical look.

"No, nothing." Mark tried to resist it but easily gave in. "Okay, he was the first person I ever kissed. It was a long time ago, and we wanted to know what it was like. That was all, though. I swear."

"Did you like it?" Jeordie asked. Mark thought back to the night that Trevor had slept over. They were barely in middle school. They had never told, nor questioned, each other about their orientation. The knowledge had always been there between them.; So one adventurous night in the dark, they tried it out. They had never done it again, but Mark figured if anyone was going to be his first, it seemed right that it was Trevor.

"I liked kissing. Kissing him seemed a little strange, though, almost like kissing my brother," he admitted.

"I wouldn't mind kissing your brother. He is cute," Jeordie half-teased. Mark gave him a playful shove. "I'd rather kiss you." They both leaned in and their lips met. For a split second, the world fell, and there was only soft warm bliss. After a moment they quickly broke away and checked to see if anyone had seen them. The field remained empty; even the sun had almost completely hidden itself away. Mark leaned in again, but Jeordie stood up instead.

"I have to go. It's getting late."

"Yeah. Me too." Mark reluctantly stood as well.

"So we're on for tomorrow to study?" Jeordie asked conversationally, as if the kiss never happened.

"Sure. Sounds good," Mark said, confused. He was picking up mixed signals.

"See you tomorrow then." Jeordie started to walk off, then turned and said, "We'll probably have the house to ourselves for a little while." He raised a conspiratorial eyebrow. Mark couldn't stop his grin. He had been chasing after Jeordie since last spring. Trevor may have been right; he wasn't the cutest guy in school, or the smartest, but Mark liked him anyway. Maybe it was because he was such a stark contrast to his best friend. Trevor was wild in comparison to just about anybody. He put out the appearance as a good boy who only rebelled in family-friendly ways. His hair was a little longer than most and he always wore that biker jacket, but he had all the adults fooled into thinking that he was nothing more than a fine upstanding young man. Mark knew different.

Trevor gave him his first beer, offered him his first cigarette, and constantly tried to convert missionaries to "the other side." At first it troubled Mark to see his friend go down such a destructive path, but he realized that the boy wasn't bad, just trying to spread his wings a little in this repressive place. Mark rationalized that an occasional smoke or a little alcohol on a weekend was different that a week-long meth bender or a twelve-pack every night. Plenty of that could be seen around town despite Grason being a Mormon-dominated area. The status quo tried hard to keep its environment family-friendly, which Mark didn't mind so much. He saw nothing wrong with family-friendly; he just didn't care for the cloud of denial and ostracizing that hung over everything. He couldn't openly be himself. It grated at him. Instead he tried to satisfy himself with the knowledge that he would go off to college, like Isaac did, and he could be free.

Trevor, on the other hand, let it crawl under his skin until he became defiantly erratic. It explained the occasional drink, the occasional toke, the occasional flirt. If Mark were to be completely honest with himself, he would recognize the small ember of jealousy. Jealous of Trevor's easy rebellion and jealous of the guys he had made out with. Mark was a virgin, and he knew that Trevor was not, and he did his best to not feel somehow left out by that. He tried to reason that it was the town's fault. The atmosphere was too repressive, and there was an invisible but tangible line. On one side was God and family; on the other was hopelessness, drugs, and white trash. The "bad side of town" appeared indicative of that, but it was through Trevor's adventures that he found out the invisible line ran just as easily through neighborhoods such as their own.

Grason was, at its heart, an agricultural town. And with that came the desperate hold of its small town values. He understood why people left. He understood why Isaac left. Even if it was to an equally morally oppressive place as BYU, at least it was a change of scenery. He worried about Trevor sometimes, hoping he wasn't getting in over his head, but he understood it and was a little envious. He wished he could let go like that, but even the few rules he did break, he felt guilty and paranoid the entire time.

He thought about his kiss with Jeordie and his mood brightened. Finally able to spend a little time with each other, he felt content. He had grown tired of the only interest he received being via text message.

IV.

"Well, it's about time one of you made a move, I guess," was Trevor's response, days later, when Mark told him of his study session with Jeordie. "So have you two spent much time together since?" He had a definite lack of enthusiasm in his voice.

"We studied over at his house yesterday after school," Mark said in a hushed voice as they stood by his locker. He didn't want anyone to overhear. School gossip rarely stayed in school. It was usually taken to Seminary classes to percolate, then to church to grow and expand.

"I'm sure you did study, just not math." Trevor adjusted the strap of his backpack with practiced sullen grace.

Mark felt his face redden slightly. "We made out for a minute. He was afraid his sister would walk in on us."

"I hear she's a freak. She might like to watch."

"Jeez, Trevor! You have issues."

"All I'm saying is that if I was into that sort of thing, I'd totally go for her." Trevor said and Mark believed it. If he would have been honest with Trevor,

29

or himself for that matter, he would have admitted that he found her more distracting than he anticipated during his time there. Stacia Ward was three years older than her brother and had graduated the year before. She still lived at home and worked at a nearby Dairy Queen. She had black-dyed razored hair and a couple of visible piercings. He imagined that her father, Coach Ward, had a conniption when she came home with those. He meant to spend time with Jeordie but Mark found his gaze lingering on Stacia anytime she was in the room.

"If you were into that sort of thing," Mark said, trying to deflect himself from his own feelings.

"I'm into that sort of thing," a female voice said from behind them. "And I'd be careful of what you say around here." The boys turned to see a short button-nosed blonde standing there. "The infamous Hannah has returned," she said sarcastically.

"More like nefarious, from what I heard," Trevor said. "So they decided to let you back into the general population."

"My parents had to decide what was worse: a potential lesbian or high-school dropout."

"Did you convince them that a lesbian drop-out was worse?" Mark asked.

"More or less. I'm still under 'house-arrest,' though. To school and home and church. No stops in between." Hannah was always a little acerbic in tone, but Mark could sense a change. Her words held more of an edge to them than they had before.

"Have you had a chance to talk to Lindsey? No one has seen her since 'the incident,'" Mark asked carefully.

"No, I haven't. Apparently I'm akin to the devil in her parent's eyes, and I tried to bring her on board to some evil gay agenda. They actually went so far as to pull her out of school. She's going to school in Cache now."

"What? Really? They drive all the way out to some little hick town just so she can go to school there?" Trevor couldn't believe it.

"Yeah. It sucks."

"So, you two were friends for years. Was there always something there or what?" Trevor asked bluntly.

"Like you two haven't kissed before?" Hannah gave them a crooked brow. Mark instantly looked around to make sure no one heard; Trevor just laughed. "We were close. Then we got closer. It wasn't like we were boning or anything." She turned to go. "Be

31

careful who you associate with, boys. I'm sure they are already suspicious of you for just talking to me."

"Hopefully this blows over and you can see her again," Mark said.

"Hopefully? Heh, you're funny." They watched her walk off. Wordlessly they pointed themselves to the exit and home.

V.

The cool afternoon bit at their faces as Mark and Trevor walked across the soccer field after school, each lost in their own thoughts. Their encounter with Hannah days before lingered with Mark. For some reason he wasn't able to shake the conversation from his mind. Was what she said true? Was it really as hopeless as all that? Mark didn't want it to be. He wasn't happy about hiding, but he had come to accept it. At least until he moved out. Trevor's dour face betrayed the fact that he shared Mark's thoughts. He felt like a dam ready to burst if something didn't change soon. Mark sensed it; he had known Trevor too long not to.

"Isn't that Jeordie up ahead?" Trevor pointed to the middle of the field, where Jeordie lumbered before them. Mark looked up and felt what little optimism he had vanish. "Aren't you two supposed to be all hot and heavy now?"

"I don't know. He hasn't talked to me in days. I've tried to text him, but he won't text me back."

Mark sighed. After their study session, they talked and texted; then suddenly nothing. Even at soccer practice, Jeordie barely acknowledged him. He feared he had done something wrong but had no clue as to what it could be.

"Hey! Jeordie!" Trevor called out. Mark tried to shush him, but it was too late. Jeordie turned and just nodded his head in acknowledgement before turning back. "C'mon." Trevor grabbed Mark's arm and jogged towards the other boy. Mark protested, to no avail. "Nobody ignores you," Trevor said quietly as they approached.

"Hey guys, what's up?" Jeordie said as he white knuckled the strap of his backpack.

"I hear you've been ignoring my boy here. He likes you a lot, you know. You should treat him better," Trevor said.

"Stop." Mark commanded his friend. "I'm sorry. Trevor is just being..."

"Honest," he interrupted. "Now you two love birds work it out. I'll be over here." Trevor nudged them together then walked a few yards off.

"Jeordie, look, I'm sorry about this. He's a little weird sometimes. But yeah, I guess I felt a little brushed off when you wouldn't talk to me," Mark admitted.

"You have to understand, things are different for me. I have so much....is he lighting a cigarette?" Jeordie said. Mark looked over to see Trevor hunched over, fighting to keep the flame on his lighter in the breeze. Mark swore under his breath as Jeordie continued. "Mark, listen, I've been going through a lot lately. I think that you're a great guy and everything, but we may have made a mistake."

"Mistake? Like what?"

"Like, you know, back when we..."

"Kissed? That didn't feel like a mistake. You were as much a part of it as I was!" Mark accused.

"I was confused. I didn't know what I wanted. I'm not that way." Jeordie tried to turn away but Mark wouldn't let him.

"I think you're more confused now. I can bring up two months of texts from you that clearly say you were into me. If you're just not into me anymore, then at least be honest and tell me. Don't give me this 'I'm confused' bull."

"Please delete those texts. It's not you, okay? I really was confused. I thought I liked you. I guess I did, but I don't like guys. I'm not that way, and I'm sorry I led you on."

35

"I don't believe you. I think you're just scared."
Mark growled, getting up in his face. Trevor flicked his
cigarette and took a step closer. He had never seen
Mark like this before. "I think you got spooked when
Hannah came back to school."

"No, it has nothing to do with her. I was going
down a dark path…."

"Don't you dare give me that crap. The last
thing I want to hear is some Sunday analogy. There
were some honest feelings there. If you don't feel that
way, then fine, tell me. But don't even tell me that
suddenly you're straight." Mark's face burned hot with
an anger he didn't even know he possessed. Rejection
was one thing, and he felt he could handle it as well as
anyone, but it hurt more to be rejected because of
someone desperately trying to lie to themselves.

"I'm not allowed. Please leave me alone. It's
all just a lie." Jeordie gave him a shove. Mark recoiled
more from his words than the contact. "Whatever it was
you thought, you thought wrong."

With no warning, Trevor's fist shot forward and
connected with the round-faced boy's chin. Another
punch flew, and suddenly Trevor landed on top of him,
the teenagers rolling on the ground the ground

pummeling each other. Mark stood scared and helpless, unsure what to do. He wanted to disappear, but all he could do was stand there and watch the fight. He heard a yell from the other side of the field and tried to call the fight off. Finally he rushed in and pulled Trevor off. Judging from Jeordie's face, Trevor clearly came out the victor.

"C'mon, we have to go," Mark pleaded. Trevor stalked after him, panting.

"You can't live a lie forever," Trevor called back and then spat on the ground.

"What choice do we have?" the defeated boy said.

Mark and Trevor quickly walked away. Mark held a stunned silence as Trevor grumbled under his breath. Trevor hadn't beaten anyone up since they were in grade school.

"That dick," Trevor finally said aloud. "He strings you along for months and then suddenly gets cold feet. What an asshole."

"I'm sure he's not the first to come to the brink then suddenly shy away," Mark said with a sudden sympathy that surprised even him.

"You're going to apologize for him? And stop talking in allegories. I'm not in the mood for that crap."

"Listen, it's not like coming out grants you a parade. Some people get overwhelmed by it and go slinking back. I mean, yeah, I liked him, but now that I know who he really is, I'm glad it didn't go farther."

"Still, he shouldn't have played with your emotions like that," Trevor grumbled.

"Thanks for looking out for me," Mark said and gave him a mock bow. He was appreciative of his friend, regardless. Trevor always looked out for him, and it meant the world.

***

The house sat wonderfully empty when Mark got home. He immediately slumped into his Dad's chair, remote in hand. He hoped they wouldn't get in trouble for Trevor's fight, but he had a feeling Jeordie would keep his mouth shut. If he was so scared of the wrong questions being asked, he'd keep this to himself.

The phone rang. Mark answered it reluctantly.

"Hey, little brother, what's up?" Isaac's voice said from the other end.

"Nothing," Mark said.

"Mom and Dad home? I'm sure they're mad because I haven't called in a while. You know how it is with the college life."

"Nah, they're both at work still."

"Okay, so what's new with you?"

"Nothing," Mark said with little enthusiasm. Isaac's exuberant tone grated on his nerves.

"Talkative, aren't you? You sound depressed. What's up?" The exuberance of Isaac's voice was replaced with concern.

"Nothing," Mark repeated. Mark and Isaac always got on as brothers do, sharing secrets and rivalries. Mark, for his part, remained the more distant one.

"C'mon, what is it? Girlfriend break up with you?" Isaac teased.

"No."

"Boyfriend break up with you?" Isaac teased again. Mark didn't say anything. "If there's something you want to talk about, you know I'm here for you,." he said seriously.

"You wouldn't understand. So are you on the Dean's list, the star quarterback, and dating the head cheerleader yet?" Mark said, changing the subject. It came out less teasing and more snarky than he was aiming for.

"Not yet, but give it time," Isaac said, letting it go. Mark knew his attitude had been getting more barbed as the time for his brother to leave for college neared. He hoped Isaac didn't take it too personally. "Listen, I'm serious. If you have anything you want to talk about, I'm here."

Annoyance at his brother being "perfect" again rose up in Mark. He wanted to talk to someone other than Trevor, but he had no idea who he could trust. "I'm good," he said. "Just been a long day."

"Something is wrong. I can tell." Isaac's ability to see right through him only helped to lower Mark's defenses.

"It's just that….I dunno. It's hard to say," Mark said then paused again, unsure what words would convey what he was feeling. He suddenly missed his brother so much. The mixed emotions he had when Isaac left for school were replaced by an empty absence. "I really wish you were here right now. There's a lot I want to tell you."

"I'm here right now. What's on your mind?"

Before Isaac could finish the sentence Mark heard the key in the door. In walked their mother, her briefcase in hand. Walls that had started to recede crashed back into place, and Mark sighed. Whatever he might've admitted retreated back behind that wall.

"Isaac's on the phone," he said to her. "I'll talk to you later," he mumbled into the receiver. Excitedly she took it as he walked to his bedroom. He flopped onto his bed, even more depressed than before.

VI.

Trevor rubbed his hands together in anticipation. Carefully he typed in the code to get past the net nanny. *As long as my parents keep coming up with these unimaginative passwords, life is good,* he thought. He sat there for a moment, wondering where he should go first, but time was of the essence. His parents would be back soon. He quickly pulled up the website he wanted and unzipped his pants. He made sure the door was closed.

He had the volume up only as loud as he needed. He still wanted to be able to hear when his parents came home. Time slipped by as he got lost in the writhing flesh on the screen. Lost in the actions on the screen, he failed to hear the front door open and shut. When his mother opened the door, he panicked. The split second deer in the headlights look gave way to immediately bending over to cover himself. His reaction was not fast enough to close the screen before she saw the two naked men together.

"Mom! Jesus!" he screamed, scrambling for the mouse. His father came stomping I'm behind her.

"Trevor, watch your mouth," he said before

42

coming to a full stop. He took one look at the monitor then said in a low voice, "Go to your room." One hand holding up his pants, Trevor quickly ran off leaving behind the muted sound of sex and embarrassment.

He lay across his bed, his heart pounding in his chest and his face burning red. "I am so screwed," he said to no one. In the living room, the TV came on and the volume was raised up. "Yep. Screwed." When his parents turned up the volume, that meant they didn't want him to hear what they were discussing. Long minutes went by. He strained to hear their voices but gave up and paid attention to the news coming from the television instead. More unrest in the Middle East. On the domestic front, Congress refused to agree on anything.

After twenty long minutes, Trevor carefully opened the bedroom door and called out, "Can I come out?"

His father stood up, looking at his son only briefly. Trevor saw a dull anger in his eyes. Anger and disgust. Without a word, he put his hand on the doorknob and closed the door again.

Trevor resigned himself to his purgatory, expecting the worst. His mother would yell and cry; his father would explain what he did wrong and struggle to contain his anger. But this wasn't just getting in trouble again. Yelling would be the least of his worries. There were grown men committing carnal acts on that monitor when they walked in. He readied himself for the possibility of violence tonight.

Trevor lay back down on his bed. A familiar helpless feeling crept over him, and he hated it. His father constantly tried to dictate his life while his mother tried to smother him with the easy way out. She always told him that if he didn't think he could do something then it was okay, don't worry about trying. All he heard was that he shouldn't bother because he was going to fail anyway. Anger quickly consumed the helpless feeling, another commonplace reaction. Because of the anger, he so readily went headlong into situations that weren't "proper living", according to his parents. If a little high or a little loving made him forget the anger, then he couldn't see how it was bad. At least he wasn't starting fires or touching kindergarteners, he reasoned.

Finally the anger grew too great. He flung himself off the bed. He couldn't take it anymore and had to get this over with. They could leave him alone all night if they wanted to, and all he would do was stew. The time had come to have the conversation with them that he should have had long ago. Opening the door, he stepped into the living room. His father stood up again but Trevor stopped him.

"I'm not going back into my room. We need to talk," Trevor said as his father's face flushed. His father's hand began to raise.

"Aaron, please," his mother pleaded feebly.

"Sandy, don't start. Son, go back into your room. I'll call you when we've decided what to do with you," His father said.

"You can hit me all you want. I won't stop you. We are going to have a talk that is long overdue. Then you can decide what to do with me." His father sized him up for a moment then sat back down. Trevor sat on the couch, his mother hugging the far end. No one said anything for a moment.

"I don't blame you. You were curious, and that's fine," Sandy started cautiously. "Sometimes you have to look something in the face before you realize how bad it really is."

"No, Mom. I wasn't looking at gay porn because of curiosity. I was 'curious' at eight years old. Now I watch it because I want to bust a nut," Trevor said.

"Watch your mouth." Aaron warned him again.

"It's the truth, and that's what we need to talk about. Not that you walked in on me watching porn but that you walked on me watching porn with two dudes. I'm gay! I like guys!" Trevor thought he would feel more relief finally saying those words to his parents, but it didn't feel any different. The words meant nothing if they fell on deaf ears.

"You are confused. You are sixteen years old, and that's still an impressionable age. I let you wear that jacket and have the hair. Maybe I am to blame for giving you so much freedom. I've let you go too far afield," his father said. "I just wanted you to have some room to grow while staying on the right path."

"Dad, there is nothing wrong with me. I haven't strayed anywhere. I'm the same Trevor,." he said.

"We've heard rumors about you, son," his mom said, tentatively touching his hand. "We've heard you might have smoked drugs, and your dad found an empty beer bottle buried in the trash. Curiosity is fine, but you have to understand it's a slippery slope."

"Your mother and I think that you've fallen in with a bad crowd, or maybe that damned internet has infected your mind. We think you need some help. This gay thing is just confusion."

"I'm not confused!" Trevor said jumping up. "I have never been less confused about anything. I like to be with guys. I love the way they feel. The next chance I get I'm going to do it again. I don't need you to tell me what is right because I know it isn't wrong!" he raged as his father's expression never changed.

"Sit down," Aaron commanded. Trevor continued to stand. "We will get the help you need. No son of mine is like this. Whatever we have to do to beat this devil, you can bet we'll do it." To Trevor that sounded more like a personal threat.

"God loves you, son, and we love you. Please feel that in your heart, let it take this darkness inside you away," Sandy pleaded.

"So I'm just a dirty sinner?" Trevor goaded her.

"Yes. You are, and we will rid you of that sin."

"Or what?" Trevor continued to push. He wanted a final resolution now. There weren't going to be months of tense dinners and furious prayer sessions. It had to end now.

"There is no 'or what,'" Aaron stated with barely hidden anger.

"Or? What?" Trevor challenged him one last time.

"A higher power lives in this house, and if you can't abide by that, then maybe there isn't room for you."

Trevor looked back to his Mom, but she just stared at her nervous hands. "Fine. Fine!" He threw his hands in the air and stepped back. "Fuck all y'all! I'm out, and you won't have to worry about me anymore. You two and God can get all sorts of cozy. I don't need this." Big hands grabbed the scruff of his neck and spun him around. His cheek stung before the open hand even touched it. He recoiled, and tears sprang to the corners of eyes. His mom sobbed once and crawled into herself some more.

"This is my house, and you are my son," his father said through clenched teeth. "I will not tolerate any of this...attitude...this backsliding from the

Lord…this complete disregard for myself or for your mother. Get back into your room and straighten up."

Trevor stood almost eye to eye to the man, but his entire life he had felt so much smaller. He didn't feel smaller now, but it didn't matter anymore. Man and boy stood their ground, waiting for the other to move first.

"This is who I am. Either accept me or don't," Trevor said quietly.

He watched the muscles in Aaron's jaw work. Sandy sobbed again as she watched her husband ball up his fists. She knew what was next. So did Trevor. He stepped back then walked around his parents and back to his room. Instead of throwing himself on his bed like normal, he slipped on his leather jacket and dug out an extra pack of cigarettes he had hidden away. He marched out of his room towards the door.

"If you walk out that door, you won't be walking back in." Aaron bellowed.

"Is that how you really feel about your only son?"

"Get the hell out of my house," he yelled.

Trevor wrenched the door open and stepped out; leaving it wide open as he stomped away from the place he had always known as home.

VII.

Mark lay on his bed reading, still trying to decipher his own personal meanings in *Dahlgren*. Something tapped at his window; he ignored it, thinking it was the wind. Something tapped again, this time with a recognizable cadence. He looked up, surprised to see the shadowy visage of Trevor's face pressed up against it. He sprang from the bed and opened the window, the chill fall night invading the room as he did.

"What the hell are you doing?" Mark asked.

"I'm Elder Buell, and I'm going around checking houses in the area to make sure no one is touching themselves inappropriately," Trevor said.

"You just missed it. I was using both hands and a feather. But really, what are you doing here?"

"Can't a friend call on another friend in the middle of the night?" Trevor said.

"Geez, man, you gotta go home." Mark started to close the window again, but Trevor put a hand out to stop him.

"I can't....I was kicked out. Can I come in, please?"

51

Mark stepped aside as Trevor clumsily clambered in. "What happened?"

Once the window had been quietly closed Trevor told him about the argument he just had with his parents. "So I guess I'm homeless now," Trevor ended.

"That is crazy." Mark had always known how hard-ass Trevor's parents could be but never dreamed they would actually kick him out of the house. "What are you going to do?"

"I was hoping I could crash here tonight," Trevor said, giving Mark his best impression of puppy-dog eyes.

He relented. "Okay, but you have to be quiet. If my parents hear you, they'll wind up calling your parents," he warned.

"Yes, sir." Trevor gave an exaggerated salute. As he swung his hand back, he accidentally knocked a model rocket off a nearby shelf. It fell with an audible thud. Trevor whispered an apology as a voice from the hall way called out.

"Mark? You okay?" His mother's voice was at his door. Trevor picked up the rocket and put it to his hips, thrusting phallicly.

"Yeah, Mom. I just knocked something down," Mark called back, trying to swat the toy from his friend's hands.

"I thought I heard voices," she said as she opened the door. "Oh Trevor. I didn't realize you were here." She noticed his hips just as he stopped and let the toy fall back to the floor. "It's late. You should go home."

"Sorry, Mrs. Jensen. I was just leaving." He turned to climb back out the window when Mark stopped him.

"Can he stay the night?"

"Aren't you a little old for sleepovers?" she asked suspiciously.

"Yeah, but…." Mark hesitated.

"It's late, and I'm already here. I promise you won't hear a peep from me," Trevor said.

"Okay," she agreed reluctantly. "I'm going to call your parents to make sure they know you're here."

"They know I'm here, so you don't need to call them. I told them I'd probably stay the night."

Clara gave a severe glance toward her son. "And when were you going to tell your Dad and me about this?"

"Sorry." Mark apologized.

"Dig out the air mattress, and I'll grab a spare blanket. Next time, let me know when you plan something like this," she said and waddled from the room. Both boys sighed in relief.

"Are you scared?" Mark asked. The air mattress lay inflated and empty on the floor. Trevor lay next to Mark in his bed. Side by side the boys stared at the ceiling in the dark.

"Naw. I have a few people I can crash with until I figure out my next move."

"You could stay here. I could talk to my parents."

"Are you crazy? Once they find out what happened they'll banish me for life." With no answers in the dark, conversation stopped. Each boy lay there with his own thoughts. "I am a little scared about all this. I'm glad you let me in because I could really use a friend right now."

"Of course." Mark told him. "After all you beat up my almost boyfriend for me. It's the least I could do. You smell like an ashtray, by the way."

"That's the smell of manliness. Now shut up and cuddle," Trevor said.

Mark put his arm around his friend. He wondered just how much comfort he could offer when he was just as scared. What would he do if he was ever kicked out? Could he survive on his own?

***

Mark jolted awake as his bedroom door flew open. His father stepped in, and Mark panicked; he couldn't be seen in the same bed as Trevor. Too late. Trevor rolled over and opened his bleary eyes, realization coming only seconds later.

"Trevor, you should probably go," LaVell said, his expression betraying little.

"Can it wait until after breakfast?" Mark asked while wiping the crust from his eyes.

"I'm sure he'll be fine. Get dressed."

The boys emerged from the bed as he left the room. It wasn't lost on Trevor that the door was purposely left open.

"Shit," Mark mumbled.

"He must have called my parents," Trevor said as he put his shoes on. "I won't be allowed over here anymore."

Wordlessly they emerged from his bedroom. His mother stood at the kitchen counter, wiping at a spot long since clean while his father waited in the living room. At the front door Trevor looked back.

"Thanks," he said to the Jensens.

"There will be no other sleepovers," LaVell said with a set-stone finality.

Trevor nodded his head and then said to his friend, "I'll talk to you later."
Once the door shut behind him his mother shuffled into the living room. "No he won't," she said, sharing the same final tone as her husband.

"What's going on?" Mark asked.

"You know full well what's going on. I called Trevor's mom this morning. She told me all about his tirade last night. That boy needs help," she said.

"After that phone call, to find you two asleep in the same bed...." LaVell shook his head.

"We don't want that sort of influence on you. You have a bright future ahead of you, and we don't

want to see him tarnish that in any way. Your dreams
of getting into college and working at NASA are not
going to happen if you hang out with the likes of him."
Mark couldn't look at his father as he spoke.
Frustration built upon itself.

"It's not like that. I know Trevor isn't a saint,
but it's not like he's a demon either. He had one night
where things got out of hand. He's learned his lesson."
The defense he built for his friend's case fell on deaf
ears, and he knew it.

"It doesn't matter. You are not to associate with
him any longer. It's pretty apparent that he's not a
healthy influence on you," LaVell said.

"Did you know that he was a homo?" Clara
interrupted as she moved into the living room.

Mark didn't answer immediately; he his
mother's surprising vehemence gave him pause. "I did.
I've known for years. So what?"

"He slept over almost more that he slept at his
own home all that time, that's what. In all that time, if
he did....did he do anything...did he try to make you do
anything you didn't want to do?" Clara grabbed at the
recliner and shakily sat in it, emotion over coming her.

"No! He's my best friend, not some pervert."
Mark started to shake.

"He is a pervert, and he freely admitted it."
LaVell said.

"It's not perverted to like boys! There is
nothing wrong with it!"

"Watch your tone young man. You're on thin
ice, and I don't know what sort of ideas he's put in your
head. The Bible clearly defines the sin," LaVell
continued.

"It can't be right about everything," Mark said,
knowing he couldn't win this fight but plunging onward
anyway. "It also says that half the stuff Mom does on a
daily basis is a sin, but I don't see you castigating her."

"I'm not the issue. We're concerned for you,
and that is completely different," Clara immediately
countered. Mark's argument caught in his throat.
Attacking his pregnant mother wasn't going to be the
best tactic.

"What if I were to say that I was gay too?
Would you kick me out like Trevor's parents did?"
Mark asked quietly. His parents hesitated only a
fraction of a second, but it might as well been a
lifetime.

"You're not, so it's a moot point," his father said.

"No. What if I were to tell you right now that I like guys? After all, you did find me in bed with another guy. What would your reaction be?" Mark pressed. Everything in him screamed to shut up. This was a stand he had been too terrified to even envision, but here he was pressing on despite it.

"In that unlikely event, you would need help. We would help you turn back to Him before you acted upon it and thought became sin," Clara said. She wore a steely gaze that Mark had never seen before. Any shreds of hope that his parents would have understanding and acceptance had vanished. They would ask Jesus, and Jesus would have other people's words answer for him. Despite what he had been taught all his life, he now realized that those words never really cared for him.

"I guess it's good that you have at least one son that's not messed up then, huh?" Mark took long fast strides to his room, slamming the door behind him. LaVell stomped after him but his wife put a hand on his arm as he passed.

59

"These are the trials. These are the tests that the Lord gives us. And leave your brother out of this!" she yelled after him. "This is such a hard age." She said to her husband. "We need to take care of this before he's led down a bad path."

"You're right. But you don't need this in your condition." He sighed. "We need to work this out."

"We do but as a family."

"Mark. Come out here," LaVell called. When his son didn't emerge, he knocked on the bedroom door, and then opened it. The room was empty expect for a high-pitched whistle from a window that wasn't latched properly. When he returned to the living room, his wife already knew.

"Let's go find him. He can't be far." She struggled to stand but he put a hand on her shoulder.

"Give him a chance to blow off some steam. He'll come back."

"He's a good kid, but so impressionable. I worry about him," Clara said, her hand resting on her swollen belly. "And her."

VIII.

Buttoned up against the cold, Mark walked briskly and aimlessly. He subconsciously tried to get himself lost, to find something new and unfamiliar. Everything familiar to him felt like a betrayal. He had lived in Grason his entire life, and it had always been home. It didn't feel like home to him at the moment. It felt like a suffocating and hostile alien environment. His head roiled with conflicting thoughts and emotions. One thought would slip into another before it had a chance to form properly. Anger, fear, and confusion made him a ball of nervous energy. He shook slightly from it, and he jumped every time a car went by.

He wandered, directionless, and when he did look up he found himself standing at a stoplight downtown. The old, turn-of-the-century buildings crammed together, reaching out but never reaching up very far. As he crossed the street he worried that his parents might be out looking for him. Ducking out of the cold, he entered a music store. The cloying sweetness of incense assaulted him, and his skin prickled from the sudden warmth. Behind the counter, a bored twenty-something gave him a half-hearted greeting.

Mark absently scanned the racks of second-hand CDs and dusty vinyl records. Paying little attention to his surroundings, he accidently bumped into the only other patron in the place.

"Oh, sorry," he said, finally looking up from a Supersuckers CD.

"Hey Mark," a tall brunette said. She gave him warm smile.

"Hi Jennifer. I didn't know you shopped here," he said, lamely trying to be polite. Conversation was the last thing he was up for right now. He had shared classes with Jennifer since elementary school. They had been close acquaintances in that friendly "stuck in school together" sort of way. Jennifer had always gone out of her way to say hello or be in group projects with him. He appreciated it because she was smart and easy to talk to, but the fact that she had been harboring a long suffering attraction to him wasn't lost on him either. For years he had always told himself that if he wasn't gay, he wouldn't mind going out with her. Lately, when he spied her in the hallways or in class, a distant voice would whisper in his head to ask her anyway.

"I come in here sometimes. Really, I'm just here because I'm bored and waiting for my little sister next door." She shrugged. A family salon sat next door, and it catered to the freshly coifed Sunday crowd. "I suppose you heard what happened to Trevor," she said. She had a hint of sympathy in her voice.

"Jesus. Bad news travels fast around here."

"No. I bumped into him a little bit ago. He didn't look so good. I think he might have been drunk or something."

"Yeah, probably." Mark didn't question where he would have gotten inebriated this early in the day. It was Trevor, and what he wanted he got. Maybe Trevor wanted to get kicked out. Trevor was never much for being confined. Did Mark want to get kicked out too? Was he that similar to his best friend? No, he decided. He wasn't nearly as impulsive; he needed to know where his feet were going to land when he jumped

"Where was he?"

"I saw him at the gas station, trying to panhandle a cigarette." Jennifer saw the hope in Mark's eyes, so she added, "I don't think he's there anymore. Sorry."

"Thanks."

"You okay?" Jennifer asked. "You seem a little distant."

"Yeah, I'm fine. It was good seeing you, but I have to go. See you in class," he said and hurried out. An idea occurred to him. Aunt Caryn wouldn't be able to locate Trevor, he knew, but he felt he could talk to her. He dug around in his pockets and realized that he was missing the usual weight of his cell phone. That was fine; he didn't have too far to go. It was Grason after all.

***

Mark knocked on his aunt Caryn's door. She answered it, pleasantly surprised to see him. Once inside, she could tell something was wrong. She sat him on the couch and disappeared in the kitchen to make some instant cocoa.

"So, what's on your mind?" Caryn asked.

"I got in a fight with my parents. They found out about Trevor being gay, and we got into it," Mark said looking around. Caryn's house was similar to his own in layout and decoration. A few pictures of religious inspiration adorned the wall; the rest were of family. Above the television hung a shelf full of framed photographs of his Uncle Steve. It didn't seem that long ago that he and Trevor would go on fishing trips with his father and uncle. Now that all seemed so far away.

Caryn handed him a steaming mug. "Do you miss him?" she asked.

"Yeah. I was just thinking of the fishing trips we used to take," Mark said and then took a test sip.

"I used to love those trips because I got the house to myself for the day," she said with a sad smile. "Now I get I have it to myself all the time."

Mark didn't know what to say. Instead he took more sips of his cocoa.

"Tell me about this fight. You're obviously pretty upset about it," Caryn coaxed.

Mark took a breath then explained what happened with Trevor getting kicked out of his house and crashing in his room. When Mark admitted that he tried to come out his parents, she stopped him.

"Hold on. You tried to come out to them?"

"I asked them what they would do if I was gay. I thought they would get the hint."

"Mark, adults aren't mind readers. If you mean something, then you need to say it. They're just going to think you are acting out," she counseled.

"So you think I should just come out and say it?"

"Well...I don't know. You've already opened the proverbial Pandora's Box on that one. But you could close it back up again before anything gets out. It might not be the right time."

"What do you mean? I should just keep it hidden now?"

"Your parents love you, but they aren't the most understanding. I just think that this might not be the best way to do it."

"There isn't a best way to do it. I've been terrified my entire life to tell them the truth. Now it's all I want to do."

"Then ask the Lord." She made it sound just that easy.

"I don't think that will help. According to everything I've been told, Jesus isn't on my side on this one."

"Thoughts are one thing. That's not the sin. It's the action."

"So you're saying that I'll be all right as long as I keep it hidden for the rest of my life?" He sat his cocoa down. A new emotion was beginning to emerge, one he couldn't immediately identify.

"No, that's not what I'm saying. All I'm saying is seek some council on it. There is a group…"

"Oh I know that group." Mark said bitterly. "They meet in the basement of the church and try to pray the gay away. I refuse to do that because I know I'm not wrong." He finally recognized the other thing he was beginning to feel. It was betrayal.

"Mark, that's not what I'm saying. It's something completely different," she started but could see that it wouldn't do any good. Adolescent stubbornness had taken over. "I'm on your side here. We just need to work on the best way to deal with this."

"I appreciate it, Aunt Caryn, but I really don't think that's what I need," he said before standing up to leave.

"I'm trying to help. You can't do this alone."

"Does this group meet in seclusion and talk about how not to be gay?"

"Well…I suppose, but that's not the point."

"Yes, it is. It's the point exactly." He let those words hang in the air as he left.

After a moment she stood up and poured out his cup in the sink. She was worried about him, more now than ever. Cursing herself, she had hoped to explain what she really meant before he stormed off. She rinsed the cups and put them back in the cupboard.

"I'll give him a couple days to cool down, and then we'll try again. He's a smart kid, just angry and scared," she said to the pictures of her husband as she stood in front of her small altar to him. "I'll do anything I can to help him."

IX.

The next few days were long and miserable for Mark. He dutifully went to school but couldn't concentrate on much. At home he lived like a phantom, spending all the time in his room except for meals. At the table they all ate in uncomfortable silence, no one looking at each other. What little conversation did happen between his mother and father usually consisted of the impending arrival of his new sister, Rachel. Any questions directed at him were short and direct. Once he finished eating he hid in his room again.

He hadn't talked to Trevor since the morning his parents kicked him out. He worried about his friend. Trevor didn't do well at making long term plans, and Mark worried that he might be sleeping on the street or worse. He had asked around school if anyone had spoken to him, but no one had.

In the hall between classes, Jennifer walked up to him. "If you haven't heard from Trevor yet, maybe we can go looking for him after school. I'm sure you know of some places he likes to hang out."

"Sure. I'll meet you out front," Mark said. It seemed that no one noticed or cared that his friend was gone. "You have a car, right? There's a place in the foothills that he liked to go with the boys' church group. He might be up there."

"We'll check it out. I'll meet you after school."

The rest of the afternoon crawled by. He tried to will the clock to move faster. Mark had a mission to find his friend. It would be nice to be away from home and his parents as well. These last few days he relished soccer practice, but the season was nearly at an end. He needed new excuses to stay away from home. And though he was unable to admit it, he wanted to spend some time with Jennifer as well.

The final bell rang, and he bounded from his seat. He rushed to the front of the school. Jennifer already stood there waiting for him.

"So did you want to go straight to the foothills or check some other places first?" she asked as they walked to her car.

"I've already looked everywhere else. It's the only other place I can think of. I appreciate this, by the way. You seem be the only one who has noticed or cared that Trevor is gone"

Mark knew of only a few friends who Trevor might stay with. When he wasn't at any of those, Mark blew off a soccer practice to search all the areas the homeless people stayed: under the overpass leading out of town, a couple of well populated alleys, and even the homeless shelter hidden away in the warehouse district. No sign of him anywhere. He tried not to be hurt that Trevor hadn't tried to contact him.

"We can get up there and back before dark," Jennifer said as she unlocked her fading hand-me-down Honda. Mark slid into the passenger side, setting his backpack at his feet. As they left the parking lot, Jennifer said, "You know, I wanted to talk to you anyway. Since the thing with Hannah and Lindsey happened, and now Trevor, it has to be difficult for you."

"What do you mean?" he said, forcing himself to keep looking forward.

"You're gay. I know it, and its fine. I'm guessing your parents don't?" she said. Mark merely nodded. "Well, I mean, we've known each other since we were in grade school, and we were never close friends, but we got along, right?"

"Yeah. That's true." Mark could sense that she was leading up to something but wasn't sure what it was.

"What I'm trying to say, I guess, is if you need to keep your, you know, cover from getting blown, sorta…I mean, I could help," she stammered, then took a breath to gather more steam. Her words tumbled out before she lost the nerve.

"It can be hard to be 'out' in this community. Look what happened to Trevor. We could 'date,'" she took her hands off the wheel and added the air quotes, "as a cover. You could actually date whom you wanted, but publicly it would look like we are."

Mark didn't answer immediately. The silence made her face redden. Finally he said, "I appreciate what you're trying to do. It might make things easier on me, at least publicly. Yeah, my parents would leave me alone, but it wouldn't be right. Would you be able to date who you wanted to?"

"I'm not worried about that," she said.

"It wouldn't be fair for you. Plus, it's more than that. As much as I have to already hide who I am, I don't want to live in a complete lie."

"Oh." She said trying to not show her hurt feelings.

"You're amazing to suggest it. It's something no one else would do, and it means a lot to me," he told her. The sentiment touched him, and he didn't want her to feel bad about it. Being jilted by Jeordie still preyed on his mind, and the thought of relationships had left a bad taste in his mouth. His life had become complicated, and even if it wasn't a real relationship, per se, this threatened to make it even more so. *But if that was the case then, why does my chest tighten a little at the thought of it?*

Before he could linger on it, his cell phone rang. It was his parents. He let it ring, contemplating whether or not to answer it. Finally he said hello.

"I need you to come home right now," his mother said in a tight voice.

"Why?" he didn't mean for it to sound impertinent, but it came out that way.

"It doesn't matter why. Come straight home. We need to talk."

"I have something I need to do. I'll be home soon," Mark said irritably.

"No, you're coming home right now." His mother's voice had an almost frantic edge to it. He hoped that she was just over-emotional due to the pregnancy. He agreed and hung up.

73

"I'm sorry, I have to go home. My parents are having a fit. Thanks for offering to take me up there. Maybe tomorrow?"

Jennifer turned the car around and drove him to his house. "You think he might have gone all the way to Cache? I have a cousin that lives there. I can ask him to keep an eye out," she said as Mark got out of the car.

"It can't hurt. I don't think he'd go there, but it's worth a shot. Thanks." They exchanged goodbyes, and Mark could see the look of disappointment in her eyes.

As soon as Mark walked through the front door, he knew something was wrong. His parents sat at the table, making a point not to look at him. His first thought was something had happened to Trevor.

"What's wrong? What happened?" he asked.

"Put your stuff away and sit down. We need to talk," his father said.

Mark obeyed. He walked into his room and tossed his backpack on the bed along with his jacket. He noticed it was in more disarray than usual. Further inspection revealed that someone had gone through his room. Dresser drawers weren't shut completely, and even his mattress sat slightly askew.

"What the hell?" He stormed out.

"Sit down." LaVell commanded. Mark did so with a thump. "Your aunt was just here. She mentioned some disturbing things that the two of you have been talking about."

The betrayal he felt before surged back up again. She had no right to come here and talk to his parents about him. "What did she say?" Mark asked through his teeth.

"You told her that you were gay," Clara burst out. "Why would you say something like that to her?"

"First off, she had no right to tell you that. What I told her, I said in confidence. Secondly, yes I am gay. I tried to tell you that days ago. I am gay. There I said it." He had finally said the words to his parents he had been so scared to. The weight of the secret that sat on his chest didn't lighten. If anything, it only became heavier.

"Don't say that," Clara said, struggling to stand.

"Mark, you've just been mixed up by your friend. Trevor was a bad influence on you and has you all confused. It's a phase," LaVell said.

"Dad, I've been attracted to guys since I was seven years old. I'm pretty sure it's not a phase."

"You have nothing to be angry about, son. These thoughts aren't a sin, they are just a test. These are growing pains in a very trying world. There is so much negative influence now. We want to help you before you act on it," LaVell said. "You haven't acted on it, have you?"

"Jeez, really? Just because I'm gay you think I'm some sort of nymphomaniac?"

"It's a phase. You are not gay," LaVell said again. "With the internet and all these pop stars that look like twelve year old girls..."

"That has nothing to do with it." Mark's voice rose to a level he had never dared before with his parents. "And Mom, lime Jell-O will not solve this."

Clara stopped like a deer in headlights as she emerged from the pantry with a box of Jell-O mix in her hand. Apparently deciding that it might, she continued to the counter and began digging for a bowl.

"Son, you are confused. Maybe it's Trevor's doing? He has your head all twisted around, thinking that sin is salvation, but it's not. You are my son, and you are a child of God. I know that you are a good person, and so does your mother. This will pass."

"So I was a good person until you found out that I was gay?" Mark said in a quiet tone.

His mother stopped and turned around while his father continued, "Of course that's not what I mean. You are a good person, and you are not that way."

"I am gay. Therefore, by your own words, I am not a good person. That is what you just said." Both of his parents started to protest, but he cut them off. "I am repeating what you said, but you're not getting the point. With every fiber of my being, I know who I am. If you want to blame anything on Trevor, blame him for allowing me to be honest with myself."

The room became uncomfortably quiet for a moment, everyone's eyes avoiding each other. Anger had replaced the fear inside of Mark. It burned hot as he realized there was going to be no winner in this argument. And with no winner, they would all lose.

"Mark, we love you. Your father wants only the best for you and for you to find happiness. We're just afraid that you're making a rash decision due to negative influence," Clara said in a quiet, caring tone. She finished with the Jell-O and took a seat opposite him at the table.

"Yeah, one negative influence in particular," LaVell mumbled.

"Jesus, Dad! Lay off of him!" Mark yelled, the hold on his anger slipping.

"Mark! Watch your language," Clara admonished.

"Am I really that bad of a person? Just a dirty sinner? I was born this way, and that means the Heavenly Father made me this way. How is it such a horrible thing if I'm the way that God made me?" He jumped up from his chair and paced the dining room.

"It's just a trial," Clara said.

"Like hell it is. I've just heard two things. I'm not bad, but I'm going to hell. They contradict each other. How can a person live like that? Is it better to just live a lie and go to heaven? When I face the final judgment, they will look on me and tell me that I told only one lie in my life. That lie will be my entire life."

"Mark we're just trying to help. You have to understand, this isn't just how we feel, it's the church. We're worried about your well-being and your soul," Clara tried again.

"Son, I need you to sit down," LaVell said, his voice quiet and forceful. When Mark didn't comply, he slammed his hand down with a powerful clap on the table. Clara jumped, and Mark reluctantly took his seat. "Listen carefully. You may think you know what's best, but you don't. You are not some deviant. What you think you know is wrong. It's just confusion. We will deal with this, even if you have to start going to church in the evenings. You will also sever all ties with the Buell kid."

"And if I don't?" The question hung for long seconds.

"I don't remember your father giving you any other options," Clara said with finality. "You need to get straight with God, and I'll be damned if you are going to bring this taint to your unborn sister."

"Is this how you feel too?" Mark asked his father.

"Mark, this isn't healthy for your sister. I don't want her coming into the world with this."

Shaking with rage, Mark stood up and walked to his room. He carefully shut the door behind him and sat on the bed. It felt as if his skin couldn't contain all the frantic emotions surging and crashing. He just sat there and breathed.

"Son?" LaVell called at the door.

"What?!" Mark screamed at him.

"We're not done with this." He walked off as Mark imploded. He silently screamed until hoarse sounds tore his ragged throat. He sprang off the bed and picked up a trophy to hurl it against the wall, instead he slammed it back down on the dresser. Slumping down on the bed, he stared at the floor, crushed by defeat. Tears welled in his eyes as he deflated. All the rage and sorrow gave way to despair.

X.

Mark lay on his bed trying not to think. The argument with his parents had left him a jumble of nerves. All he thought he knew left him scared and confused, angry and hurt. His stomach rumbled, but he refused to step out of his room for food. If he never faced them again, it would be fine with him. He heard the faint murmur of their voices from the kitchen table but tried to ignore them. It wasn't until he heard his name more than once that he got off the bed. He took an empty glass from his nightstand and put it up to his door.

"LaVell, I don't want this getting out," Clara said

"I don't either, but there is a group that meets at the church. Maybe it wouldn't hurt if..."

"No. I don't want this getting out," she repeated emphatically. "This is our problem, and we'll deal with it. Besides, it might hurt my business. And I really don't want to be lumped in with the Buells'. Why did Mark do this to me?" His mom's tone stung him. She was treating this like some sort of personal offence. As if he chose this way as a slight against her.

"We can't keep him cooped up in the house the entire time. The Robinsons having been doing that with Hannah and are already having issues with her sneaking out." His father's voice carried hopelessness. Mark couldn't understand where it came from. He was the same that he always was. Unless they always thought he was hopeless, that he would never measure up to his brother, and this was just the final nail in the coffin.

"I pray that my parents never find out. They wouldn't know how to handle it." Clara paused, and then said slowly, "He is our son and I love him, but I don't know if I want this sort of thing in the house with Rachel so close to being born. She will be so defenseless against that sort of degradation." His mother's words filled Mark with ice. He stood in chilled shock.

"That's my other concern. You're so close to having her that I don't think this sort of strain is healthy for you or her." They were quiet for a moment, and Mark held his breath, waiting. He seethed as he did, almost to the point of tears. The blood in his veins began to catch fire. "Should we tell Isaac?"

"No. He doesn't need to know about any of this. School should be his priority. When he comes

82

back home on break, this will all be settled. One way or another," Clara said, and Mark couldn't help but feel it was a threat. "Maybe we can't handle this. At least right now. We're going to be so busy with the baby soon."

"Meaning?"

"Meaning we remove this blight from the house now."

His mother's words bit into him and refused to let go. He took the glass from the door, unable to listen anymore. One thing had become clear to him; he was no longer wanted in his own house. A cresting wave of emotions crashed into him, and it fueled one singular desire: leave. He had never had the compulsion to run away in his life. Now he might not have any other choice. He put the glass back up to the door, desperate for a respite. But instead he heard silence. Obviously their minds had been made up. The silence killed him, but in that silence he made a decision. He no longer wanted to be where he was no longer wanted. He filled his backpack.; Anger and betrayal overcame fear. He packed clothes and a couple of paperbacks. He took a wad of twenties from a tin on his dresser. He had only saved about hundred dollars from allowances and odd jobs. He'd have to make it last.

Once packed, he sat on the edge of his bed. *I'll find Trevor*, he thought, *and together we can come up with a plan. Maybe we can stay with my Aunt?* He immediately dismissed the idea. She started this mess when she opened her mouth to his parents. With a shuddering sigh he waited until his parents went to bed.

The wait was excruciating. He felt himself start to doze when his phone buzzed on his nightstand and jolted him awake.

"Hello?"

"Hey there, fellow packer of fudge," Trevor's familiar voice sang in his ear. Mark checked the number but didn't recognize it.

"Where the hell have you been?"

"Aw, you were worried about me. That's sweet." Trevor spoke slowly.

"Are you high?"

"Maybe a little. I don't have parents to worry about, so screw it."

"Well, neither do I. I'm sneaking out of this damned place as soon as they're asleep." Mark proceeded to tell him what had happened. "If they don't think I'm fit to live around my own unborn sister, then I don't need them," he finished. Trevor's giggling on the other end didn't help his mood.

"Dude, we've both outgrown our parental situation. Where are you planning to go?

"I have no idea, but I'm leaving before they have a chance to kick me out." Mark didn't have a plan at all. The best he could do was crash at one of his mom's empty houses, but that would just be for the night.

"I have a guy. You can stay here. I'll ask him, don't worry. Get your stuff together, and I'll be there in about an hour."

XI.

Mark looked around his bedroom. This had been his room for as long as he could remember, and every square inch of it, every object it contained, threatened him with memories. He tried to wipe away all the firsts that had happened here: the first time he realized that he could turn his fascination with space into his future, trying on his first soccer jersey, his first kiss. His first kiss had been with Trevor, and now Trevor waited for him outside. There was something disturbingly poetic about that.

He put his cell phone on his nightstand. He didn't want to be tracked by it. If they didn't want him, then there was no sense in trying to be found. Closing the door behind him, he wanted it to feel poignant, but really it happened out of habit. How many times had he and Isaac chased each other in the hallway? Straight ahead, he saw the kitchen window they broke when he failed to catch a passed football. The living room was filled with images of church meetings, opened Christmas presents, lazy afternoons with the whole family fighting for control of the television. Each memory now carried a burden and that burden now a lie. The unquestioning trust and love that he'd assumed the walls held were false. He had grown up in a false-led life.

In the movies the person would set the bag down and take one last look around before walking out the door into a bright new day. He let his momentum carry him forward because he knew this wasn't a movie. If he set the bag down, he would never pick it back up again. He had no bright new day waiting for him, just a chilly moonless night ready to swallow him up. Trevor sat on the front step waiting for him.

"Now what?" Mark asked. It was an existential question. The question spanned both time and space. By stepping over the threshold of this front door, he had committed himself to a course of action that scared the hell out of him. Every step he took from here on led to a dark unknown.

"I told you, I'm crashing on this guy's couch. He's cool, don't worry. He said he'd pick us up at the school, so we should get going." Mark followed his friend, now the only one he could put his trust in. He hoped he hadn't put it foolishly.

They stood in the dark by the football field. Minutes passed and the chill air penetrated his coat.

"So who's this guy you've been staying with?" Mark asked.

"Just a guy I've done some business with before," Trevor said. Mark knew that "business" meant "bought weed from." A two-tone Ford Taurus pulled up in front of them. Muted thumping music surrounded it as they walked towards it. Trevor opened the passenger side door, and Mark was greeted by the sounds of Sublime. The skinny driver, in his mid-twenties and pockmarked, had a crooked mouth and suspicious eyes.

"Hey man," Trevor greeted him. "This is my friend Mark." The man extended his hand, and Mark shook it with a mumbled hello. This was all it took, and the driver's demeanor lightened.

"Nice to meet you. I'm Luke. Get in." Trevor immediately sat in the passenger's seat while Mark carefully climbed in the back. "Sorry about the trash. You can just move it over," Luke apologized. Under Mark's feet crunched various fast food containers and Mountain Dew bottles.

"Thanks for picking us up," Trevor said while Mark sat watching the lights whizz by. Fear welled up inside of him, cooling his veins and tightening his chest. He just wanted to get through tonight.

"So are you staying at the house too?" Luke asked breaking Mark's reverie.

"Um, yeah, I guess so," he answered hesitantly then gave Trevor the evil eye. He had *just* run away from home and Trevor hadn't even bothered to ask the guy yet?

"Mark's cool. He's clean and quiet. Just don't get him started on space crap. He'll prattle on all day about it," Trevor replied.

"That's cool. I like astronomy and all that. You know about the planet that's on the other side of the sun? It's actually coming towards us but the governments don't want anyone knowing about it."

"Um," was all Mark could comment on it. He hoped Luke wasn't serious about this.

"See, the government knows all about it. They don't want to say anything and cause mass panic. Plus they are in communication with the other planet. I shit you not. You know SETI?" Mark said yes, he had heard of the organization that was devoted to communicating with life outside our own planet. They were doing science, though. He wasn't sure he wanted to hear what insane theories this guy had about them.

"Those guys at SETI have been talking back and forth with the planet. It's called Nibiru, and the population is hyper-advanced. They intentionally moved their planet's orbit so it flies by the earth."

"That would cause an amazing amount of damage to both planets," Mark said against his better judgment.

"That's the thing; the inhabitants are dug in underground. When the planets fly by each other, we'll have all these disturbances, and then the governments will finally be able to combine and subjugate us. Same with Nibiru. Once they go by us, they'll sling shot Mars, come back around, and stay in our orbit. That is what they wanted in the first place. They were too close to the sun before."

"Dude, it'll just crash into us if we have the same orbit," Trevor interjected.

"No, no. It will be the same orbit, but different position. Like ahead of us or behind us, get it? Just have its own place in the same orbit around the sun." Luke was talking animatedly, obviously enjoying the display of his theory.

Mark didn't want to tell him that gravity didn't work that way. Or the million other things wrong with his ideas. Instead he replied, "I see," hoping to end the conversation.

"This kid is cool. You guys can stay, but only for a couple days. Then you have to figure something else out. Having a couple runaways isn't great for business, and my girlfriend isn't crazy about people staying over," Luke told Trevor.

"That's all we need, and then we'll be out of your hair," Trevor assured him.

Mark hoped that he could find the same confidence his friend had. They pulled up to house that had seen better days. It wasn't in a real disrepair, but in the dark, the discoloration of visible paint layers could be seen. Luke unlocked both the knob and two deadbolts before they were able to walk in. The house was uncomfortably warm in contrast to the chill outside. A sickly sweet smell hung in the air. The furniture was ill-kept and gaudy rent-to-own, from the print couch to the giant television across from it. The black and gold coffee table held soda can rings, worn game controllers, and overflowing ashtrays. On the television, *Law and Order* blared.

"You can show him where to drop his stuff, right?" Luke asked Trevor.

Trevor nodded and led Mark down a small flight of stairs into a carpeted basement. It was sparse, containing a ratty couch and a severely scratched wooden coffee table. The far wall was lined with cheap metal shelving crammed with brown boxes. "Here we are. Luke let me stay here if I cleaned it up. Not too shabby, huh?" Mark didn't know what it had looked like before, but he was just impressed that Trevor was able to clean anything. His room had always looked like the aftermath of a riot. Heavy footsteps preceded Luke as he joined them. He had a small tin box and a six pack of Coors in his hands.

"I'll let you guys fight over who gets the couch and who gets the floor." He set his things on the table and plopped on the couch. "I just want you to know, I hold no prejudice. Just because you like guys, it doesn't bother me any. I'm a live and let live kinda guy. I sell to all kinds, and as far as I'm concerned, everybody's money is green. Right?" He guffawed. "Doesn't bug me one bit. Just don't start fucking on each other while I'm sitting here," he warned, a smile still on his crooked lips. He handed a cold can to each teenager and then carefully opened the tin box. Trevor eagerly popped his beer open and took a noisy sip. Mark looked at the yellow can in his hand before opening it up and carefully taking a sip. It wasn't the first time he had tried beer, but it was the first one he had all to himself.

While they drank, Trevor and Luke began talking about something funny Luke's girlfriend, Janelle, had said earlier. Mark wasn't paying much attention; he became oddly mesmerized with watching Luke pack dull green leaves into a glass pipe blown with colors of green and blue. Mark took a quick sip of beer, then another one. Luke tipped a red Bic to the bowl of the pipe and lit it. A sweet burning smell filled the room. Trevor took a long inhale then held it out to Mark. He hesitated.

"What? It's not like you have to worry about your parents smelling it on you," Trevor coaxed him.

After a moment, Mark took it and the lighter. He took a long drag only to explode in a fit of coughing. Luke cheered him on as he took it from his hand. The smoke clung to the air around him.

As they took drags off the pipe and sips from their cans of beer, the anxiety that held Mark started to get further away. It sat there still, ever present, just a little more distant than before. As his head began to swim, he leaned against the wall. His body was both tense and relaxed at the same time; he wasn't even sure how that was possible. His eyelids got heavy, and before he knew it, the sounds of conversation had lulled him to sleep.

***

He woke up in the morning on the floor with a moment's panic as he didn't recognize anything. He saw Trevor snoring lightly on the couch, and then it all came crashing down on him: overhearing his parents' conversation, the decision to leave home, and the numbing uncertainty of anything beyond this moment. *All I have is loss of everything.* But then he changed his mind. *All I've lost,* he thought, *was a family willing to throw me away and a church ready to condemn me.*

He refused to cry. *This wasn't my fault,* he reasoned. On that poorly vacuumed floor, he asked God for an answer. He demanded an answer. No answer was coming. The voice of all his family members and hundreds of devout church goers echoed in his head. *This is a trial. You are being tested*, they said.

"Fuck your test," he whispered at them. Trevor stirred then sat up, sleepily stretching.

"Sleep well?" Mark asked him sarcastically.

"Yeah. You sure knocked out quick," Trevor said. Mark agreed with him. He was a lightweight and he knew it.

"So, now what?" Mark asked him.

"I dunno. We crash here for a couple days, then we get out of town. Go somewhere new."

"Like where?" Mark asked, but Trevor just shrugged by way of an answer. Above them were the sounds of life. "How well do you know Luke?"

"Well enough. Good guy for being straight. Bought weed from him and then started hanging out. I told him my sob story and offered to do whatever odd jobs so I could get a couch to stay on for a few days."

"This guy isn't going to kill us in our sleep is he?" Mark tried to make it sound like a joke.

"Relax." Trevor stood, leaving the couch a mess of blankets while Mark quickly tidied up.

Upstairs, Luke sat on the couch, setting the tare on a small electronic scale. "You guys want some breakfast?" He opened a box of pizza that sat on the coffee table. The boys each took a slice of Hawaiian. Trevor gobbled his down while Mark attempted to make his last a little bit longer.

"Is it cool if I make some coffee?" Trevor asked. Luke just nodded as he worked.

Trevor and Luke chatted as the man worked, weighing and bagging. Mark sipped at his over-sugared coffee. He didn't say much. In fact, he felt perfectly content with being invisible, to just be part of the furniture while the other two chatted happy as you please.

Once the pizza and coffee were gone, Luke said, "Listen, I hate to do this, but you gotta go. My girl put her foot down. Staying here a few nights is one thing, but taking in one more stray did it for her, I guess. Plus I got someone coming over soon. He gets paranoid with other people around. Sorry."

Trevor stood and jovially said, "No worries. I appreciate the use of the couch and letting my boy Mark crash here last night. Once I get a little money, I'll be calling on you."

Backpacks in hand, they walked out into the afternoon. They made it to the end of the block, each one looking up a different end of the street.

"I suppose we could go to a shelter. Technically we're homeless," Mark suggested. He tried to think in the most helpful terms he could. It kept back the ragged fear.

"The only shelter I know of is run by the Church. We walk in there, and they'll call our parents because we're minors."

"We can sneak into one of my mom's homes. But we have to leave first thing in the morning in case she has an early showing," Mark said.

"Let's find a fancy one. I always wanted to crash in a fancy house." Trevor started to trot across the street, leaving his friend a little disturbed by how much Trevor enjoyed this.

In the cold night Mark shivered. Trevor sat next to him against the bare wall, his head bobbing in sleep. Mark used his arm as a pillow, the musty smell of the carpet filling his nostrils. They had grabbed a meal of dollar burgers and fries and waited for dark to fall.

97

Mark knew of a home that had been on the market for months and no one had shown interest in. It was the safest bet they had, at least for the night.

Sleep wasn't forthcoming. He blamed the cold and the hard floor. The truth of it was he was too keyed up from anxiety and fear. His mind refused to shut down. All he could think of was that they had nowhere to go. School was out of the question. Though they hadn't spoken of it, it was agreed that they had not only runaway, but they didn't want to be found. Trevor assured him that they would work something out but always neglected to say how. What hurt Mark the most was the feeling of being unwanted. His parents, whom he had always assumed would take care of him, didn't want him. He had feared their reaction if he had come out to them, but this was not the reality he envisioned. Even his Aunt Caryn, who was more open-minded, left him with a bitter taste of betrayal. How could she have thought outing him was a good idea?

Hot, fat tears rolled down his face as he quietly sobbed into his arm. All the fear and pain came at once. With the idea that they might wind up living on the street and the possibility of everything he envisioned for his future being gone, the first bittersweet flavor of hopelessness came out. It seemed so unfair to him. He hadn't harmed anyone in his life, had honored his family and honored a higher power. Maybe he didn't go along with everything the Mormon Church decreed, but he always had a strong faith. Why was it that he and Trevor were now sleeping in an abandoned house in the middle of October, he wondered. Why must it be so hard to just try and live an honest life?

XII.

 A busy week had passed since Mark left home. When his parents realized that he had gone, they waited. It never occurred to them that he might be capable of running away. As day turned into night they started making discreet phone calls as to where he might be, including one awkward one to Trevor's parents. With no luck, they realized Mark didn't want to be found. LaVell reasoned that their son just wanted to "teach them a lesson." Clara wasn't as optimistic.

 After twenty-four hours had passed, they contacted the police and reported him missing. A search was undertaken with fliers and alerts. The police asked them a lot of uncomfortable questions that they could only shrug their shoulders to. They didn't know why he had left. Possibly under an unhealthy influence, they postulated.

 In the afternoon of the fourth day, two Child Service representatives knocked on their door. They were there only a short time. When they left, LaVell grew red in the face and Clara quietly seethed. The questions had started routine enough—general info about the home and Mark as a person. Steadily they became more invasive about how they disciplined and what sort of weapons were kept in the house. LaVell and Clara became flustered when they were asked if they regularly beat their child or if there were any instances of sexual abuse.

"We have only love in this house. And with that love, a straight path to heaven," Clara said, as offended as a person could possibly sound. This seemed to satisfy the social workers. Unable to contain herself, she also added, "You might want to pay a visit to the Buells'. It might not be sexual, but I'm sure there was some kind of abuse going on over there."

The social workers stood. "We've already been over there."

The taller of the two said, "I know this is hard, and we apologize again for these questions, but they have to be asked."

Her companion replied as they showed themselves out, "You folks just worry about getting your boy back."

"It was their boy that took ours away," Clara said.

"We aren't comparing you with the Buells. You have a fine house, ma'am. And at least you didn't refer to your child as 'that little faggot.'" The social workers left. Husband looked at wife, reading the expression on her face.

"What? Well, he is. It's a shame our boy is mixed up in his business."

***

The church gathered around them with comforting words and promises of action. Flyers were posted and the search was started for Mark. Caryn pressed the fact that Trevor had been missing as well when it looked like the search became one sided. The Buells reluctantly added their son to the search. Due to her sister's condition and what she perceived to be emotional stress on the part of the parents, Caryn led the effort to find her nephew and his friend. By Sunday morning, the boys were still missing, and Caryn had growing misgivings.

"How are you doing, sis?" she asked Clara after church services.

"About as well as can be expected. I'll be better once Rachel is born. I can't sleep, and my back has been killing me." Clara sighed.

"What about Mark? How are you doing with all of that?" she pressed.

"I pray every day. I can't see why he did what he did. I just hope that he comes back to me safe," Clara said.

Her sister held back a frown. It was a generic statement that Clara had been telling people for days now. She tried to reason that it was simply something to say to all the people that asked the same thing, but it should be different with family. It should be honest.

"We'll keep up the efforts, and we'll find him," Caryn said and put a sympathetic hand on her shoulder.

LaVell stood by quietly. He hadn't said much since the ordeal started. As they walked to their car across the church lawn, Caryn watched and debated. She had started having uncertainties right after she had found out that Mark had gone missing. She watched her sister and brother-in-law do all the things they were supposed to with a runaway child—call the police, pray, gather family and friends, etc. But she couldn't help but feel that they were just going through the motions. After two days, they both went back to work, letting her take care of all the logistics of the search. Even now, the police used her as a point of contact. Was this all obligatory? she wondered. Maybe all for show? She hated herself for even questioning her sister's intentions with her own son, but she seemed to have everything but emotion.

Their refusal to tell Isaac unnerved her the most. At first she understood that they wanted to sort things out before worrying him. It was now apparent that Mark was missing on purpose, and his only brother deserved to know. Slowly walking towards her car, she made a decision.

Once home she sat on her couch and dialed her eldest nephew's cell phone. Maybe he would know something that would help the search, she reasoned as it rang. A dark thought emerged behind it. What if that was the reason they didn't tell him? She shook it away as Isaac answered.

"Hey, Isaac. It's your Aunt Caryn."

"This is a pleasant surprise," he said.

"I know I probably wasn't the girl you were hoping to call you," she tried to joke.

"You're my favorite girl," he said, always the flatterer.

"Listen, kiddo, I don't want to worry you, but something's happened, and I feel you should know."

Hesitantly at first, she explained that Mark had run away, possibly with his friend Trevor, who had also disappeared. Isaac asked about the police and what was being done. She tried to keep her real feelings to herself the best she could.

"I've never lost a child, so I can't say that what I feel is justified," she explained. "It's just that they seem....distant."

Isaac didn't say anything for a moment then asked, "Did Mark tell them that he is gay?"

"After the kerfuffle with Trevor, he tried. I don't think they wanted to hear it, so they dismissed it. I only managed to make it worse." A gnawing doubt which she had thus far been able to ignore came full bore. If she hadn't confronted them about Mark's sexuality, maybe he would have never left. If anything happened to him, she would never forgive herself. "Mark confided in me a while back, and I confronted your parents about it. I thought I could make them see reason," she confessed, but she only felt worse for it.

"Mark has always been an honest person. I don't see how he could keep it to himself much longer. Don't blame yourself. It was going to happen eventually." Isaac had genuine sympathy. "Last time I talked to him, I think he wanted to come out to me, but we were interrupted. It's been hard this last year. It almost felt like he didn't like me anymore, but for a moment, on the phone, I think it had fallen away."

"You don't think your parents kicked him out, do you? This whole search is just a smoke screen?" The question tasted horrible on her lips.

"No. I don't know if they would actually kick him out, but between God and appearances...I don't know. They couldn't want him to just stay away, would they?"

"Of course not," she consoled both herself and her eldest nephew. "They love him and want him to be safe at home."

"Yeah," he agreed. "I'm coming home. I'll find a ride up there."

"No. Stay in school. Besides I don't want your parents to find out I said anything to you," she said quickly. She felt she had done enough damage. Reluctantly, he agreed and said good bye.

Isaac sat on the edge of his bed in his dorm room and stared at the phone in his hand. Next to him were a stack of textbooks he needed to study. He had already blown them off; he wouldn't be able to concentrate on school work now. His little brother was missing. He knew that wherever Mark was, Trevor was too. *At least he's not alone,* he reasoned, *but Trevor isn't the greatest influence.* But it wasn't Trevor that worried him the most; it was the unknown. There were too many unknowns.

Caryn had her guilt, and he had his own. It didn't matter whether it was justified or not, they carried it anyway. He knew Mark had wanted to talk, and he should have pressed it. He had reasoned there would be another time. But what if there wasn't ever another time? Despite his promise to his aunt, he made a decision.

The door opened, and his roommate, Jackson, walked in with his tie askew on his Sunday finest. "Hey, man. Why so glum?"

"Do you know someone with a car? Someone willing to take me north?" Isaac asked him.

"Um, yeah, Bennett has a car. He might drive you if you have the gas money. Going home?" Jackson asked.

"Yeah. Something's come up, and I need to get home. It's kind of an emergency."

"He's in his room. Let's go get him."

"Give me a few minutes. I need to make a call first." Isaac stood and left the room as he dialed his parent's house. He would force them to tell him. It seemed very important to him that they tell him what was going on and not to hear it second hand. Plus it would get Aunt Caryn off the hook.

"Hey honey," his mom answered, unable to hide the weariness in her voice.

"Hi Mom. Can I talk to my brother? I have to ask him something."

"He's...not here right now. He's at soccer practice," she said, obviously choosing her words carefully.

"Where is Mark? Where is he really?"

***

The Albertson's dumpster yielded a meal of dented cans of fruit and some stale bread. As the two boys sat huddled in the dark shadow of it, they quietly ate. Even though they still had Mark's money, Trevor thought dumpster diving for food would be an adventure. In some weird way it turned out to be, and Mark popped another canned peach into his mouth. His fingers were sticky with syrup, and he licked them clean before an over the shoulder toss put the empty can into the metal dumpster at his back.

"Nice shot. You should have gone for basketball instead of soccer," Trevor said with a mouthful of stale hamburger bun.

"Yeah. I thought about it." Mark looked around at the twilight sky at the end of the alley. He imagined seeing that very sky from the veranda of some fancy house. *Once this is over, I'll get back into school and then get my degree. I'll have an exquisite house with a huge veranda that will take in the whole horizon. Every day at twilight.* He continued to fantasize. *I'll come out and watch the sky turn from purple to black.*

"Hey, get your blanket from your backpack. It's getting cold," Trevor said, interrupting his daydreaming.

As Mark pulled out the quilt his grandmother had made him so many years ago, he wondered just how much of a thrill his friend was getting from this whole ordeal. Not once had he complained. Mark admitted to a small perverse sense of adventure in all this, but adventures have an end where you go back home. Or at least you have a place with a roof. The night before, they had slept in another one of his mom's houses only to be woken up by the sound of people outside. Prospective buyers wandered around outside, chatting happily about its possibilities. Standing stock still, Mark and Trevor waited until the people left. Sneaking back out, they both knew that they wouldn't be able to use the empty houses again.

Night fell, and still they sat there undetected. With a flattened cardboard box under them and two blankets over them, they leaned on each other for comfort and warmth.

"So where should we go?" Trevor asked, his head on Mark's shoulder. "Let's think of some place better than this alley." Making plans with no idea how to execute them was his forte.

"And where will we get the money?" Mark grumbled.

"Doesn't matter, we're not worrying about that now. We'll set a goal first, and then we'll figure out a plan of action. C'mon, think like a Mormon. Plan it out to the smallest detail." Trevor's smile infected Mark, who refused to look at him because of it. Finally he gave in and caught it full force.

"I've always wanted to visit the big cities. San Francisco, Seattle, Chicago, New York. Then on to Rome and Paris," Mark said, relenting.

"Rome and Paris always seemed stuffy to me. How about London?" Trevor added, keeping the game going.

"London, why London?

"David Beckham."

"He lives in L.A. now."

"Fine. Because of British punk and ancient little alleyways that have names like roads."

"That seems a little far. Why don't we pick somewhere closer. San Francisco, maybe?"

"Just how cliché can you get? Are you gay in the 80's? Let's not make it too easy for them to find us." Trevor snorted. Mark stung over the idea of someone possibly looking for them.

"If not San Francisco, then what about Salt Lake City? A bus ticket would be pretty cheap," Mark said trying to steer the conversation back.

"The only place on the planet more LDS than Grason is Salt Lake."

"Boise? No, still too close. Seattle, then." Mark thought it might be a good compromise.

"Yeah. Why not? In Seattle we will start a new life."

"A life of freedom and cavorting," Mark said laughing.

"A life of cigarettes and loose men," Trevor added.

"A life without church elders."

"A life of corrupting elders." The boys giggled and then became quiet.

"We're not sleeping in alleys. Tomorrow we find something different. Tomorrow we find an actual place to stay." Mark said it as a statement of fact, not a suggestion. The temperature had dropped, and it took his sense of adventure with it.

"I'll come up with something, don't worry." Trevor adjusted his leather jacket and then pulled the blanket back up to his chin. Mark sat there and worried.

XIII.

All day the gray sky threatened them with snow as they sat on a bench in the park. A centenarian gazebo loomed stoically next to them surrounded by dull grass. They had been sitting there all day coming up with options and ideas. At one point Mark even suggested asking Jennifer if she could sneak them in for a night. Trevor was so quick to shoot it down that it left a puff of jealousy in the air between them. Mark tried to explain how Jennifer helped search for him when he first left home, but it didn't seem to help. Trevor suggested stealing some camping equipment and going into the hills. They both had camped their entire lives and knew enough about living off the land that it sounded feasible, in theory. One thing a Mormon knew was what to do to survive. Mark pointed out that it happened to be winter and the only thing they would have to eat up there would be each other.

"What about Hannah?" Mark said taking a shot in the dark. Surely they had some friends willing to sneak them in for the night.

"What is it with you and chicks today? Why can't you think of some hot guys to stay with?" Trevor accused him.

"Because we live in Idaho. We are not a pretty people," Mark grumbled.

"Speak for yourself. Hey, what about Lindsey? What if we go to Cache/"

"She's only going to school in Cache. I'm pretty sure she still lives here in Grason."

"No, I mean I have a cousin who lives in Cache. He's a cool guy, his wife is usually nice to me, and more importantly, they have a house with extra space. I'll go call him." Trevor suddenly jumped up, excited by his idea. "They still have that old pay phone by the library?"

"Probably. I haven't got any quarters, though."

"No biggie. I'll just call him collect. I also need to find someone to bum a smoke from." Trevor bounded off.

Mark stood and walked the opposite direction, towards the gazebo. The old, painted boards creaked under his feet. Slowly he walked weighted steps, pacing as his mind wandered. Eventually he leaned against the rail and watched as fat snowflakes finally began to fall.

"We're going to Cache," Trevor declared loudly, much sooner than Mark had expected him back. Trevor exhaled smoke from a cigarette he had successfully acquired.

"How? I'm not walking there."

"We'll get a ride from Luke," Trevor said like it was nothing at all. "C'mon." Trevor led the way; Mark could only follow.

***

"Are you sure that Luke will take us there?" Mark asked as they walked up the porch to his front door.

"If I sweeten the deal he will," Trevor said confidently. Mark couldn't decide if he was envious or distrusting of the way Trevor seemed to think everything would go his way all the time.

"Sweeten it with what?" Mark asked warily, shaking the snow from this head and shoulders.

"Don't worry about it. He likes to talk about his problems a lot when he gets high, if you haven't

115

noticed. If he balks, I'll use that to our advantage," Trevor said then knocked on the door.

After a moment, Luke opened it up and welcomed them in. "What are you two vagabonds up to?" he asked good-naturedly.

Mark immediately sat on the ugly couch and tried to be as invisible as possible. This was Trevor's show; he would let him be front and center.

"Nothing, just hanging out," Trevor said nonchalantly.

Again the television was tuned to another *Law and Order* episode. Mark tried to concentrate on that, letting his mind wander in the plot of the show instead of his own reality. His reality was hanging by its fingernails to a fast moving train. He hated the helplessness of it, the fact that his life was not his own anymore. Trevor did his best to convince Luke to drive them to Cache, but he wasn't paying much attention to it. The more he focused on the television, the heavier his eyes grew. The sleepless nights had taken their toll.

He jerked awake at the sound of Trevor's voice. "Wake up. We're going. Luke is taking us to Cache."

"Let's hurry, I want to get back before my ol' lady gets home," Luke said, keys in hand. Mark stood up and stretched. Luke just stood there looking at him expectantly.

"Oh yeah, he's going to need ten bucks for gas money," Trevor said. Mark reached in his pocket and pulled out two crumpled fives.

"Thanks. Let's go," Luke said.

They piled into his car, Mark took the back seat. There was only sporadic conversation from the front seat as some suburban white-boy rap played from the car's stereo.

Trevor swiveled around and looked at his friend. "Dude, you look exhausted. Take a nap."

"It's going to be at least thirty minutes before we get to Cache. Might as well," Luke offered jovially.

Mark leaned his head against the window. Sleep sounded good. It would be a respite from reality. All it took for him was to close his eyes and he was out again.

His eyes opened again, and he was momentarily disoriented. He might have been asleep for a minute or for days, he wasn't sure. The dark landscape rushed past his window, unseen except for the occasional dots of the far off farm lights. Something seemed off. There was something going on. The energy in the car had changed. The music played, but the occupants in the front were quiet. He tried to focus when he noticed a shape slumped between the front seats.

"I'm not this way," he heard Luke explain. "I'm not into this sort of thing, but the girlfriend hasn't done this to me in years. Hell, if I even ask now, then she'll just roll over and go to sleep. I don't go for guys."

"It's cool. I appreciate you driving us out here," Trevor said.

Mark became uncomfortably aware of what was happening in the front seat. He heard the sounds, even over the music. Mark realized that Trevor had sweetened the deal with himself to get to his cousin's house. A torrent of emotions flooded him, most of which he didn't understand. It wasn't the act; it was the reasons. He knew of Trevor's promiscuousness but had never seen it in action. Was his friend so easy, or was Mark just jealous? He shut his eyes and tried to drown it out, praying for sleep again but too wired for that now. He hoped that this cousin would be worth the trip. Feigning sleep, Mark made sure his coat covered his lap. He was glad for the dark. It covered the red of his cheeks, embarrassment for Trevor and also for his physical reaction to it.

***

When they stepped out of the car, Luke gave them an enthusiastic wave then roared off in the night. Mark watched him go then followed Trevor, doing his best not to look at him.

"That was cool of him to give us a ride," Trevor said. Mark didn't respond.

A light glowed in the window but not the porch light. It did little to inspire confidence. Trevor rapped on the door. After a moment it swung open.

"Trevor? Hey, what's up? Come in out of the cold." His cousin ushered them in, obviously bewildered. Mark could see the Buell family resemblance. They shared the same shaggy-prone dark hair and pointed nose.

"Thanks Eli. You remember my friend Mark?" Trevor breezed in, and Mark shuffled quickly behind him.

"I think so," Eli said. "So what's the occasion?"

"Can't I come see my favorite cousin?" Trevor said, oozing charm. "Hey, Amanda," he called out to a tired-looking woman sitting in the living room.

119

"Keep it down. I just got the baby to sleep," she hushed him.

"How is the little guy? Must be getting big," Trevor asked in a quieter tone.

"He's good. Why don't we go in the kitchen where we don't disturb the baby?" Eli ushered them into the kitchen. They each took a piece of counter and leaned against it. Mark tried not to look as nervous as he felt. "So, what brings you here so late?"

"He didn't know we were coming?" Mark whisper-yelled at his friend.

"It's cool. We're family. But you could have let me know. I have to work tomorrow."

"Yeah, I guess I should have called, but we were close by, so I figured I'd stop and say hi," Trevor said. "Also, I had a question for you. I was wondering if we could crash here tonight.

"Isn't it a school night?" Eli asked cautiously.

"No, we're off for…." Mark started but realized that he had nothing.

"Uncle Aaron and Aunt Sandy don't know you're here, do they?"

"No. They kinda kicked me out." Trevor proceeded to spin a small and tragic tale of a misunderstanding that turned into a full-blown fight. The silky smooth lies that flowed from Trevor so easily unnerved Mark. Not once did Trevor mention the real reason he had been kicked out. His cousin listened, but Mark wasn't sure he bought it.

"Well, you can stay here for the night, but we don't really have room for you guys. Why are you here?" Eli asked Mark.

"Mark has been on his own for a while. His parents kicked him out because he's gay," Trevor said as easy as he pleased. A quick sharp anger erupted in Mark, but he quelled it the best he could.

Eli mistook the reddening of his face for embarrassment. "That sucks. You can crash on the couches tonight," he said.

"What about the extra room?"

"That's the nursery now," Amanda said coming in to the kitchen. "No shenanigans tonight. Jacob is finally asleep, and if he wakes up, then God help you."

"No worries. You'll never even know we're here. I'll even help you put the sheets on the couch," Trevor said and followed her down the hall.

Eli gave Mark a look then whispered to his cousin, "Is he cool?" Trevor assured him that Mark was no threat.

***

In the dark, Trevor stretched out on the couch while Mark lay crunched up on the love seat, his knees making a tent of his blanket.

"You're quiet," Trevor said.

"Why the hell didn't you tell me that your cousin had no idea we were coming? I thought you called him," Mark forced himself to whisper.

"I didn't have a quarter, so I bummed a smoke instead."

"Why the hell are we here? We could have stayed in Grason." Mark turned to face him.

"And freeze our asses off again? Don't worry about it. I'll talk to him tomorrow. They have a basement that they never use. I'll convince him to let us use it."

"And if that doesn't work?" Stress had made his entire body feel like a steel post. His mind raced and worried at stunning speeds. The more Trevor talked, the worse it got. "Jesus, Trevor, your homophobic cousin will have us out on our asses in the morning. Then what?"

"I got this. Don't worry," Trevor said, trying to assure him. Mark only found it more maddening. "And he's not a homophobe, just a little traditional. He'll be okay." Mark didn't bet on it, but kept his mouth shut. He was so angry that keeping quiet was his only way of getting his friend to maybe shut up. "And be careful of what you say. Amanda is like a freaking ninja. One minute she isn't there, then suddenly 'whoosh,' she's appears out of nowhere."

XIV.

A late model Honda pulled away in the front of the Jensens' house. A tall young man climbed out of it and climbed up the step.

Isaac walked into a full house. It seemed like the entire Ward congregated in his living room and kitchen. He walked in unnoticed at first. Clusters of neighbors talked amongst themselves. It was Caryn who finally noticed him. She rushed over with a large hug.

"It's so good to see you. Are you on break?" she asked.

"Not exactly. So what's going on? All I know is that Mark ran away and he might be with Trevor," Isaac said before his mother came waddling out of nowhere.

"Isaac!" she cried out and embraced him. "Why aren't you in school? It isn't break yet, is it?"

"No, Mom, it isn't. I came because my brother is missing. You didn't exactly tell me much over the phone, so I decided to come home." He tried hard to keep accusation from his voice. He'd had too much time to think on the road between Park City and

Grason. In his mind, his parents had driven his brother away. He didn't want to believe they were capable of such a thing, so he did his best to push it away.

"But your schoolwork," she chided, tears welling up. "Come sit. Your dad and I will tell you what's happened." They made their way to the kitchen, people welcoming him home on the way. "LaVell, Isaac is here," Clara called out.

LaVell turned from his conversation with Bishop Johns. "Son! What are you doing here? It's good to see you." He put a hand on his son's shoulder. Pulling out chairs for all of them, he motioned for the three of them to sit.

"What the hell is going on? Where is Mark?" Isaac sat, but it was on the edge of his seat. He was ready to start tearing apart everything to find his brother. His father started talking, beginning with Trevor and the reason that he was kicked out of his own house. As they talked, the kitchen cleared out to give them privacy. In the living room, Caryn started escorting people outside. They went willingly, knowing a family matter when they saw one. Soon the only ones left were her and Bishop Johns.

"I should probably hang back, for moral support," the round, bespectacled man said.

"We all appreciate it but we should probably give them some time. I'm sure someone will call you later on," Caryn said kindly as she led him toward the door.

"Of course," he said, smiling, and left. Once he was gone she took a place at the table with her family.

"So you are telling me that Mark left for no reason?" Isaac was asking as she sat.

"No. I'm not saying that. He ran away because of the Buell boy. That kid has a lot of problems and somehow got your brother all twisted up. I...we think that he convinced Mark to run away with him. I shudder to think what sort of trouble he has your brother caught up in," Clara said, adjusting uncomfortably in her seat.

"How exactly has he got Mark 'all twisted up'?" Isaac pressed.

"Trevor was caught...well...he's a homosexual. He's sick and needs help. I don't know if kicking him out of the house was his parent's best decision, but..." his father let it hang for a moment trying to find the right words.

126

"Either way he put some ideas in Mark's head and now they ran off," Clara finished for him.

"Mark is a smart kid. He's also very intuitive. I don't think he would be easily swayed to run away for no reason," Caryn said.

"Are you implying that we drove our son away?" Clara's voice became chokingly high-pitched.

"Of course not, sis. I'm saying that Mark must have his reasons. And whatever they are, we need to find him so we can work them out," Caryn said quickly.

A silence lapsed at the table. Clara and LaVell sat with each other, and a cloud enveloped them. The cloud was a secret. Isaac and Caryn sensed it, and in doing so a different cloud drew them together. They also had a secret. They knew the truth, or at least suspected it.

"Yes. We need to find him before anything bad can happen." Weariness crept into LaVell's voice.

Clara turned to her eldest son, "You must be hungry. I'll fix you something." She struggled to stand and went to the pantry in search of a quick dinner. LaVell gave his sister-in-law a knowing look then put his hand on Isaac's shoulder.

"I'm glad to see you, son, but how is this going to affect your schoolwork?"

"I'm ahead in everything. I told my professors I had a family emergency. They understood," he lied. His schoolwork was the least of his worries right now. After he had called his parents, he'd spent a sleepless night worrying. The next day, he convinced Bennett to drive him home with all the cash he had and a promise to tutor in Biology.

"That's good. School is important. I don't want this to hurt your grades."

Isaac agreed with them and then went to lay down for a bit and disappeared into his old bedroom. The air held the tang of paint. He parents had started turning his room into a nursery but had only gotten so far as to paint the room a bright aquamarine. He pulled off the paint-spattered plastic that covered his bed with a surreal sense of tarnished nostalgia wafting over him. His bedroom, a place that he had spent so much of his time, was now part of memories. No longer his present. A sense of unfamiliar maturity blanketed him, and he tried to shrug it off. Instead the effort made him even more tired. Flopping down on his bed, he tried to quiet his mind even if for a moment.

He finally dozed off, waking at the sound of plates clanking in the kitchen. His grumbling stomach had obviously heard the sound too. Reluctantly he stood up and stretched. He emerged into the light of the kitchen.

"Wash up," LaVell told him. "Then go get your aunt. She's outside," he said disdainfully.

Isaac knew that tone. Apparently his aunt had started smoking again. He grabbed his coat and went out the back door. She stood there by the small metal shed in the back corner of the lawn. A trail of blue smoke lazily floated up from her fingers. Walking up to her, he wordlessly took the cigarette from her fingers and took a drag from it. She gave him a wide questioning look.

"I didn't realize you smoked."

"I don't," he said and handed it back to her. "Dad says dinner is done."

Caryn nodded as she put the cigarette to her lips. "I noticed that Trevor's parents didn't show again."

"Maybe they're a little preoccupied with finding their own kid."

"Maybe. The first couple of days after they went missing, everyone rallied. After that the Buell's just drifted off. To be honest, I have no idea if they're even looking for Trevor."

"They always seemed a little harsh, but do you really think that?" Isaac wasn't ready to believe that they would just stop looking for their own son.

"Aaron Buell is a hard S.O.B. Why Sandy married him, I'll never know." She stamped out the cigarette on the bottom of her shoe and put the butt in her coat pocket. "I don't think either boy would just run off without some provocation. Trevor I understand, but Mark… something doesn't sit right with me. Let's talk about it later, though. Right now we need to eat dinner."

"What I don't get is why we aren't out tearing this entire town down looking for him." He followed her back to the house, his nervous energy returning. The need to start pounding the sidewalk and knocking on every door overrode his need for supper.

"We have been, trust me. What we can't do is search on an empty stomach." She held the back door open for him as he stepped back inside the warmth of the house. The contrast in temperature increased his worries. He hoped that wherever his brother was, it was at least somewhere warm.

***

Eli looked nervous as he sat across from the boys. Mark knew something was up. Trevor did too but wrote it off. A football game played on the television, the volume turned down as Amanda was putting the baby down for a nap.

"Hey, um, I called Uncle Aaron earlier..." Eli finally said. "I don't think you've been completely honest with me."

"I told you I got kicked out," Trevor said. "I just didn't tell you why. Does it matter? We're family."

"We're family, it's just...Amanda and I talked about it, and we don't have much room."

"Trevor said that you guys had a basement you weren't using," Mark said before realizing he was even going to speak. The thought of being kicked out again into the cold twisted in his gut.

"We do, but it's full of the stuff we took out of the spare bedroom to make the nursery. I wish I could help you. I really do." Eli talked more to the television than the two teenagers sitting there.

For long minutes the three of them sat there saying nothing and staring at the screen. "Did he say he wanted me to come back? Did he say he was going to come get me?" Trevor said, trying to get his cousin to meet his eye.

"We didn't really talk about...I mean...listen, he's your dad, and I'm sure that he wants you to come home. If you want to call him, you can chill here until he shows up," Eli said as Amanda walked into the room. She stood behind Eli, a hand on his shoulder.

"Why bother? He won't be coming." Trevor stood up. "C'mon Mark." Trevor walked toward the door, and Mark grabbed his backpack and followed. Trevor stopped and looked at Amanda, "I suppose you're happy to get the little queers out of your house."

"It's not that you're gay, it's the fact that you're just a little fuck up," she shot back.

"Hey!" Eli rounded on her, "That's still my cousin."

They didn't hear the rest. The boys walked out the door. Mark made sure to slam it hard in hopes of waking the baby up.

It was a bright gray day. At the end of the driveway, they looked up and down the quiet country road. One way seemed just as bleak as another. Mark wanted to ask Trevor about their next move, but he was tired of asking. So far all his ideas were simply brief respites from the inevitable. The inevitable being this moment, right now. They had nowhere to go, no one to go to, and nothing but barren country roads to walk down. It was only about five or so miles into Cache. He didn't know what they would do once they got to town, but it would be better than standing amongst all the dead fields.

Trevor stood there unfazed by being turned out. He scanned the horizon, a ponderous look on his face. He suddenly brightened. Mark was leery of what was about to come out of Trevor's mouth.

"I have an idea."

"Yeah, you've had lots of ideas, and so far they have all sucked."

"This one won't. Follow me." Trevor took a handful of steps down the road while Mark stood there. Suddenly turning on his heel, Trevor walked back the other direction. As he passed Mark he said, "It's this way." Mark sighed and followed him.

They walked for three miles straight ahead, then turned south and walked another three. At one point Mark had wondered if they were simply going to town.

The landscape sprawled before them. Fences cut the land, separating one brown sleeping field from another. Far on the pale eastern horizon rose the Porteuf mountain range. Under it lay the bumpy, rolling land, quiet and stark in the late fall afternoon. Here and there farm houses rose up near the worn grey roads.

They approached an old, weather-beaten farm house. Trevor paused in front of an overgrown dirt driveway fifty yards from it. As Trevor started up the drive, Mark wanted to ask what the hell he was doing, but he knew it wouldn't matter. Best just to follow and find out.

Rusted farm implements and the corpses of ancient tractors rested along the side of the rutted path they walked. Up ahead sagged a small house, more like a shack, leaning just slightly in a grassy patch. The path continued past it to a green farm gate and stubbly fields beyond.

The house sat tired and waiting for time's inevitability. The white paint had turned to a chipped gray, the red trim to faded rust. Trevor peeked in a window. He could make out the tiny kitchen. The long shadows of the day were turning into night.

"This will do." Trevor said happily as he stepped aside for Mark to look in.

"What do you mean, 'this will do'? You aren't seriously thinking of sleeping here for the night?" Mark asked incredulously. They now had only what they could carry, not even a roof over their heads. As much as he wanted to get indoors, some little bitty shack that looked about to collapse lacked appeal. He was about to tell Trevor his thoughts when he heard the screech of the door being forced open. Trevor beckoned him in through the window. With a last glance over his shoulder towards the main house, Mark followed him in.

The air inside held a creeping chill of its own. The front door led directly into the kitchen. The counters were littered with dust and bits of wallpaper that had come off in strips. The occasional beer can lay half-crushed under the battered cabinets. Venturing deeper, they came into the living room, or what used to be one. The thin carpet showed the wooden flooring underneath in tattered spots. Thick dusty curtains kept out the light. A busted and dubious couch was pressed against a wall. An open doorway led to another room where a bare mattress lay. Ahead were two shut doors. Adventurously, Trevor pulled open the first one to reveal a long neglected bathroom. Carefully Mark opened the next. The door stuck due to the neglect and extreme weather it had so long endured. Finally he yanked it open and heard the small scurrying of mice feet. The room was full of stacks of magazines and old car parts. A few tractor implements leaned against the wall.

"I guess this is used for storage," Trevor noted.

"Shame, it has a nice view." Mark looked along the opposite wall. It was almost entirely paned glass that lit the room with the gray sky. The view of the winter-dead fields and sagging fence line looked as desolate as Mark felt inside.

"That can be your room then," Trevor said, happily trotting back into the living room.

"How long do you plan on us staying here?"

"Until whenever," Trevor said with a shrug. "It's not like we have anywhere else to go, so why not here?" He let his stuff fall with a thump. The house absorbed the sound.

"We'll freeze to death. We have no food. We have no running water. The mice will eat us alive," Mark tried to reason. "I wouldn't be surprised if this place was haunted."

"You have a little money, right? We can get some supplies. Pick up some canned goods, and we'll be golden. We can get water from the farm spigot over by the pasture. It'll be fine." Trevor tried to use his patented soothing voice, but it wasn't going to work on his friend this time.

"Why don't we just go home? I can call my aunt." The situation had now gotten desperate. Maybe it was time to swallow a little pride.

"No! Bullshit! We can't go home. You said it yourself, our parents have kicked us out, and we have no home. This is our home now."

Mark studied Trevor for a moment then sighed. "What about whoever lives in the big house? I'm sure they won't want us just squatting."

"Don't worry about that. I think it's just some fat drunk farmer. Give him a few bucks and a smile, he won't care." Trevor dismissed the problem and went to dig out the old mattress dumped in the middle of the bedroom.

As he did, Mark finally let his things fall to the floor. Whether they stayed here long term or not, they needed a place to stay when night fell. If it got too bad, they could always start a small fire in the living room. Judging by the state of the place, it could use a good fire.

"We don't have much money left," Mark said, but it was a half-hearted complaint.

Now he was living minute to minute. His life led by inches instead of miles. At least they were inside, such that it was, for the night. Tomorrow rested so far away, it might as well be in a year. Tonight was all they had. Tomorrow would remain a worry for their future selves.

Trevor kicked the mattress. When nothing scampered from it, he nodded his head, satisfied. "We can roll our sleeping bags out on this. It doesn't look too tore up. I think the old bastard has been using this place for a dumping ground."

"Let's clear this stuff off. I'm exhausted." They cleaned off the debris and rolled their sleeping bags on the creaky old mattress. Mark carefully lay on top of it. The last few days had taken their toll on him and he didn't care anymore. He just wanted to sleep.

Forever maybe. If he didn't wake up again, he wouldn't have minded.

"I'm hungry," Trevor said, still standing over him.

"I don't have anything to eat, and I'm too tired to care."

"There's a gas station a mile down the road. We can pick up something there," Trevor said.

"If you want something, go ahead." Mark dug a five out of his pocket.

Trevor took it and trotted off. Mark heard the squeak of the door shut and crawled into the warmth of his sleeping bag. Exhaustion from poor sleep and a nearly constant state of stress swiftly crested over him. He yawned once then fell asleep.

He woke up disoriented upon his companion's return. It took him a moment to swallow down the fear of opening his eyes to the decaying ceiling above his head. Trevor appeared, more shadow than not, as the sun had almost completely set.

"Jeez, it got cold and dark out there. Not much better in here. We're going to have use our body heat to keep warm tonight." Trevor said, sitting next to him on the bed. "Five bucks doesn't get much. Here." He

139

handed Mark an energy bar and a large soda. "I figure we can share the Pepsi, but these should get us through the night."

He took a big bite of his own bar. Mark took a large swig of the sweet sticky soda. It crested over his tongue like heaven as cool joy washed down this throat. He wanted to drink it all at once and take it all in. Instead he handed it back to Trevor, who chewed loudly.

"How did you know about this place?" Mark asked.

"Remember a couple years ago, when my dad was trying to get me into pheasant hunting? We went tromping the fields around here."

"I'm sure you hated every minute about that," Mark said, taking the Pepsi from him again.

"I just wanted to shoot the gun. I couldn't care less about killing anything. Anyway, we didn't find anything, so we just kept walking. I think Dad got a little lost, and we wound up in the fields behind here. He went to ask up at the house if we could hunt the fields. I guess the farmer said no because we just called Eli and got a ride back. But I remembered this little house."

"Hut is more like it."

"Hey, it's better than sleeping out there," Trevor said, trying to ignore the sound of little scampering feet somewhere in the dark.

A few minutes later, they had both crawled under the sleeping bag and cuddled together. Despite the weight of exhaustion, Mark couldn't sleep. All he could smell was dust and rotted flooring. In the dark, the fears that he could keep at bay during the day came to the forefront. He didn't ask for any of this. He just wanted to finish high school quietly so he could go off to college. Once out of the house, he could live honestly. He could live, period. Now he had no choice.

Trevor shifted then turned to face him. An arm snaked over and wrapped around his chest. Mark scooted closer. He lay there staring into the darkness, almost afraid to sleep for fear of the mice, or maybe the place would just decide that this was the night it would give up and fall down on them. Trevor shifted behind him and he felt his hot breath on his neck, then soft lips.

"Trevor, don't." A thrill from the touch shot through Mark, but this was Trevor. They were just friends. Unheeded, Trevor did it again. Mark turned over to face him. "I don't think this is a good idea."

"I'm all out of good ideas." Trevor's voice cut the dark, thin and vulnerable.

Without warning, their lips met. At first Mark wanted to protest but instead gave in. In the time he had been on his own, he had felt unwanted and unloved. Maybe it started before then, with the memory of Jeordie's rejection still lingering. Though he had never been attracted to Trevor, it meant so much to feel wanted. Even more so in the dark, cold night in a tiny ramshackle farm house in the middle of nowhere. He gave in and gave back. As Trevor's hands reached for him, he welcomed it, taking comfort anyway he could.

XV.

The morning sun slowly emerged, waking the boys as it rose. They stretched and stood up. Trevor walked out to relieve himself only to come rushing back in.

"Oh shit, I think the guy from the house knows we're here."

"You fucking kids get outta there!" a deep wheezy voice bellowed from outside. The boys looked at each other for a moment. They held their breath, unsure what to do.

"I know you're in there. Get out now! It's my property, and you're trespassing!" the man hollered.

Mark gave Trevor a questioning look; all Trevor could do was shrug his shoulders. "Shit." Mark said and walked towards the front door.

He pulled it open and stepped out into the frosty morning. Gray clouds were covering the sun again. A hundred yards down the lane shuffled the rightful owner of the shack, wheezing and leaning on a beat-up metal crutch. The man was tall and bloated. His faded overalls stretched to the limit around his belly. The unkempt beard, more grey than brown, did little to hide his discontent at the teenagers. He took another step closer, obviously winded from the effort.

"What the hell happened to his foot?" Trevor asked from the doorway of the house. The man's left foot was indeed missing, the leg of his overalls pinned up.

"Diabetes, probably," Mark said quietly then called out, "We're sorry, sir. We just needed a place for the night."

"I don't care what the hell you needed. That is my property, and I don't need a bunch of damn kids using it as a party house," he said then let out a deep and phlemmy cough.

"No sir. We weren't using it like that. It was cold last night and…" Mark wasn't sure if telling him that they were runaways would be the best plan. Either way he looked at it, he didn't have a good way to get around it. They were trespassing.

"And what? You needed some little queer love den for the night?" the old farmer sneered, thinking himself funny.

"It beats doing it out in the weeds," Trevor answered. Mark shot him a warning look. He already had mixed feelings about last night, and that wasn't helping.

"Get your smart ass outta here before I call the cops."

"Okay, let's get our stuff," Mark said quickly. As he passed by Trevor, who still hung in the doorway, he mumbled, "Life just gets better and better."

He began to roll up his sleeping bag and heard Trevor talking to the owner. He prayed that Trevor wasn't out there making it worse. How much worse things could get, he wasn't sure.

"Stop packing," Trevor called out after a few minutes. "I worked us out a deal. We can stay."

"A deal? Maybe getting out of here will be a good thing. We can find a place with heat and water. Possibly less mice," Mark said, still clutching his things.

"No, this will work. We can make it work. I told him we'd do some fixing up around here for him in order to stay." Trevor beamed, obviously proud of his negotiating skills.

"That's great and all, but we need food still."

"We need a place to stay first off. This is as close as we're going to get to a home. We can fix it up a little bit. Sure, we don't have electricity, but we can live like pioneers."

"It's almost winter and already cold as hell. In a month, it will be worse. You can't be serious." Mark couldn't believe that Trevor was so adamant about staying in this dump.

"We can fix it up a little and make it home. How many high school kids do you know that have their own place? We can make some friends and have our own place with our own rules." Trevor's sliver tongue took advantage of Mark's confusion. "Oh, and I told him you'd give him rent money."

"With what? I haven't got much left"

"I told him forty now. After that, we'd work it out." Trevor said proudly.

"Fine, whatever," Mark said. He dug around in his backpack and pulled out the tin that had his cash. "Let's go." Trevor happily led the way. The old farmer had already limped back up to his house.

"You'll see. It'll be an adventure." Trevor practically bounded. Mark did not share his enthusiasm.

They reached the house and stepped up to the covered porch. It was a grimy mess of poorly rescued outdoor seating and yellowing piles of bound newspapers. Cigarette butts rolled around the ashy floorboards. Inside, they heard an epic coughing fit then an ominous silence before a thump-step, thump-step cadence approached the front door.

The farmer lumbered over and held out his stumpy hand. Mark put the crisp bills in it, and they both disappeared in a front pocket.

"The deal is you can stay in the place as long as it's just you two. That's it, though. No friends, no partying. Clean out the trash from inside it, but leave the tractor parts in the back bedroom. I still need those. If you fix up the fences in the back pasture, I don't call the cops on the runaways squatting on my property. As long as I don't know you're there, then I don't care." His gruff voice was forceful and lacking any compassion.

"Thank you, sir. We appreciate it so much. My name is..." Mark held out his hand.

"I don't care. The less I know about you damned kids the better. If I have any trouble, or just get tired of you, I'll call the cops and pretend I don't know a damned thing."

The boys politely agreed with him. Mark noticed an old kerosene heater on the porch. "Sir, does that work? We'd like to use it if it does."

Beady eyes looked at him before he said, "It's yours for another twenty." Mark thought about it for a moment before taking another twenty from his pocket. He swore under his breath as he did.

"There's a can of fuel on the back step. Once that's gone, you're on your own. Don't burn the damned thing down." And with that he slammed the door behind him. Trevor bent to pick the heater up when the door swung open making him jump back.

"And when you run that thing, make sure you leave a window open for the fumes. Otherwise you'll fucking die." He wheezed then slammed the door again. Trevor made a quick grab for the heater again and they both raced off the porch. Mark grabbed the half-empty can of gas from the back step as instructed.

Once they were back inside the little house, Trevor put the heater down. "Honey, we're home!" he called out. "You heard the man. We have to clean this place out." As campy as possible, Trevor swished from one room to the next pointing out all the places they would put their non-existent furniture. "We'll put the

148

divan in that corner and the armoire against that wall. Oh, and the curio cabinet with all the little knickknacks you love so much, it can go just along there."

Mark finally succumbed to his attempts and managed a smile. He leaned against the wall in what was once a living room. With a dusty thud he plopped on the floor. Trevor sat next to him. The house was silent except for the occasional creak and moan. It wasn't used to people anymore. Mark played with his hands, unsure what to do now. For the last few days they had been on the move. Now that they had decided to stay, even temporarily, he wasn't sure what to do with himself.

"So now what?" Mark asked. His voice filled the room with a muted echo. It only increased his feeling of disconnect from the world he once knew.

Looking around, he decided to finally take in his surroundings since he would be looking at them for a while. The living room boasted all wood paneling and chewed carpet. Against one wall, a threadbare couch that looked more dangerous than comfortable waited. A few dusty boxes sat here and there. Toward the kitchen was a dining area full of rusted metal fence posts and busted wood.

"I say we fire that heater up. It's freezing in here," Trevor said, but he didn't stand up. He didn't want to be the first one to almost burn the house down.

"No, let's save it. We'll need it more at night than during the day," Mark said sensibly. "What I mean is whatis our next step? Where do we go from here? We can't go back home. There's no one for us back in Grason, and your cousin made it pretty apparent that you aren't allowed back. You can't be serious about making this long-term."

"We can stay here until we find something else. Let's just make the best of it while we're here. How does that sound?" His leather jacket creaked as he shrugged.

"And if we don't find something else?"

"We stay here."

"Not forever. Trevor, we need a plan. We don't have much money left, and the winter is only going to get colder. We need food, we need jobs, and we need a goal. Staying in Cache isn't a plan, it's a pit stop." Mark tried not to get upset. It was becoming disturbingly apparent that his friend was enjoying flying by the seat of his pants. This wasn't what he had in mind when he envisioned moving out of his parent's house. All the uncertainty kept him permanently nervous.

"Do you think they're looking for us? I mean, they are our parents, maybe they realized they were wrong?" he asked.

"They ordered me to leave. The look in their eyes was just...disdain, disgust..." Trevor stood. "Besides, you told me yourself that your parents were going to kick you out. You saved them the effort. I'm sure they're grateful for that, at least. No awkward speeches, no crocodile tears. This is our world. We'll conquer it."

"All we've managed to conquer is an abandoned, mouse-infested house in the middle of the Idaho nowhere," Mark pointed out.

"Details," Trevor said jovially as he pulled Mark up from the floor. "We have to start somewhere, and what better place than at the bottom? We'll claw our way to the top, and when we're living large in the big city, with our fancy apartment and all your cats, they'll just be jealous."

"Why do I have to be the crazy cat queer?" Mark protested.

"Because I'm allergic, and you're already a pussy." Trevor gave him a playful shove.

The joy sat uneasily in the long empty house, but they soaked it back up as fast as they released it. They needed to laugh; there had been too little of it lately.

Without warning, Trevor put a cool hand on Mark's warm cheek. He went rigid with the touch. He didn't expect intimacy from the normally rebellious youth. His light brown eyes looked into Trevor's darker ones. For a moment, they didn't say anything.

"I'm going to take care of you. I dragged you out to this godforsaken town and into this godforsaken house. We will get through this. We don't need them, any of them." Real belief radiated from him that Mark had never heard in all the years he had known him.

"We will do this because there isn't any choice," Mark said with new conviction. If not for himself, then for Trevor. "It's the rest of our lives now."

He brushed the long hair from Trevor's eyes then leaned in and kissed him. It was a short but meaningful kiss. When they parted, Mark had to look away. This sort of closeness never sat comfortably with him, and he reasoned that it had to do with spending so much time hiding what he was from people. It made it difficult to become close to them. For that reason the kiss embarrassed him.

"You haven't kissed me since we were young. The first time either one of us kissed anybody," Trevor whimsically remembered.

Mark's face only reddened more. It had previously been the only time they had done anything other than be friends. Until last night and until just now. Mark's emotions left him confused, and he pushed them away. He couldn't handle them right now.

As Mark stepped back, Trevor flung his arms out and bellowed into the empty room, "I'm fucking hungry!"

"Let's walk into town. There's a grocery store where we can pick something up." Mark zipped his coat back up. "We need some essentials if we're going to stay here for any length of time."

"My cousin has a bunch of camping gear we can use. We can go get it later." Trevor suggested.

"I don't think he's going to let you borrow it." He had a bad feeling about this.

"Who said borrow? Let's wait until dark. By the time we get there, they'll be asleep. Besides, he owes me," Trevor quickly added, sensing his friend's reluctance. "I'm family, and he kicked me out. That's not how it's supposed to work."

The prospect of stealing something from anybody immediately made Mark scared for his future. A criminal record wouldn't allow him to follow his dreams. *All I have is right now*, he reminded himself. *No sense in worrying about a future I don't have.*

XVI.

The afternoon sun sat high in the sky as Trevor walked back into the little house. Mark worked in the cramped kitchen, sweeping up a pile of dirt and debris with an ancient broom. They'd spent the day cleaning the best they could. They had hauled out all the fencing material and heaped it in a pile outside. All the miscellaneous boxes and stacks of magazines were piled in what Trevor insisted in calling "Mark's room." He didn't mind so much, even though they slept in the same bed. He liked to sit and look out the large many-paned window. Despite the sorry shape of the place, the window was in surprisingly good condition.

With the old broom he found, Mark knocked down the worst of the cobwebs and swept up most of the detritus. Trevor cleaned off the counters but left the cabinets alone. They were both too scared to open them. On the counters sat a camp stove and a few other items acquired in the night. Mark threw his pile of dirt outside and caught Trevor admiring their newest acquisitions.

"I still can't believe we got away with it." Trevor shook his head in disbelief.

"Larceny suits you. You were like some garage ninja in the night." Mark leaned the broom against the wall and joined him.

"I have skills you don't even know."

"Apparently breaking and entering is one of them."

"We didn't break anything. The door was unlocked." Trevor mockingly defended himself, "Not my fault that Eli is too trusting. Besides, we need it more than him."

"You sure he won't come looking for this stuff?" Mark hated to admit that despite the fear of getting caught, he'd enjoyed the thrill of skulking around in the night. He had never dreamed of doing anything like that in his life.

The whole dark walk there, he just knew they were going to get caught. As they slowly opened the garage door, the smallest creak gave him a heart attack. Even his heartbeat seemed loud enough to give them away. Trevor, for his part, expertly knew his way around in the dark. They grabbed the camp stove, some small green bottles of fuel, and a large plastic water jug. The worst part was carrying it all back. The chance of

156

traffic on a back country road would be minimal, but Mark feared seeing headlights the entire time.

Despite their late night, Trevor bounded out of bed at the crack of dawn ready to clean house. His enthusiasm became infectious, and as they worked, Mark began to warm to the idea of staying here for a while. A small but delicious taste of freedom tantalized him. There might be a chance they could make this work after all.

***

Isaac sat in the passenger's side of the car, watching the yards with garish Halloween decorations pass by. He scanned the streets as they drove and tried to peer into windows of the buildings and homes for his brother. He thought they might be driving a little too fast to be looking for someone. Clara continued to look straight ahead, concentrating on the road. Despite the fact that she was about ready to have the baby, she still insisted on driving. They rode in silence except when Isaac made suggestions of streets they should turn down. He strained to look at every face they passed by. For the past two weeks, a profound depression had started to settle in on him, and he had a hard time shaking it. It had to do with more than just that his brother was still missing, which was bad enough. The attitudes that surrounded him were beginning to disturb him on a deeper level.

"We should try again at the shelter," Isaac suggested.

"I'm sure they will let us know if they see Mark. They have a picture of him," Clara said, still not looking away from the road.

"Yeah, but we should still head down there. Maybe somebody has seen him," he said, looking hard at her. She needed to look at him, to acknowledge his concern. It was important to him for some reason he couldn't explain.

"Honey, listen. We've been down there so much that it's almost like we live there ourselves. They will contact us if they hear anything." She didn't want to talk about it, but Isaac wasn't about to let that stop him.

"Let's at least go down East Bainbridge by the sleazy 'no-tell' motels. Maybe he was able to scrape up some cash and get something down there. I know Dad says he might have left town, but I just have this feeling he's close by."

"Isaac, I really have a couple houses I need to check on. I have a showing this afternoon to a nice couple and some houses that I think…people have been getting into," she said, quickly censoring herself. Her son wasn't stupid, though; he caught it but chose not to point it out. She was hiding something from him, and he wanted to catch her on it.

"Fine, we can do that. I still agree with Dad, though. You're about to give birth and don't need to be working."

"I'll be fine," she said curtly.

They rode the rest of the way in silence. Isaac grew fidgety as his brain continued to churn. He had finally admitted to himself that his parents were reluctant to find Mark, or at least ambivalent to it. Everything they did now was for show. Suppressed anger bubbled up inside of him, but he swallowed it down. The Jensens' didn't show their anger; it wasn't becoming. But Isaac had grown beyond that. The anger that dwelled in him demanded that he catch his parents in the act of ambivalence, to get them to admit that they didn't care about their youngest son.

They pulled up to a small ranch-style home on a quiet shady street. His mother pushed her seat back and carefully struggled out of the car. "I haven't been in this one for a few weeks. I may need to do a little clean up. A very sweet couple is coming to look at it. I think this would make a nice place for them." Isaac just grunted.

The empty, still air greeted them as Clara immediately went to open the blinds to let some light in. Isaac wandered around, wondering about all the ghosts of previous lives that might still reside here. People lived, loved, raged, and cried here, and he was always touched by the bittersweet emptiness of it. Houses were meant to be lived in, and once empty, they missed those lives and spent their time trying to remember until someone new moved in.

As he wandered in to the kitchen, he caught the faint whiff of stale cigarettes. In the sink were two butts. "Hey, Mom!" he called out. "I think someone has been in here." She waddled in from the living room and he pointed to the sink.

"Damn it, he was here," she said before she could catch herself.

"Who?" Isaac pounced on it. He knew who she meant, but he needed her to admit it.

"Nobody. There has just been someone breaking into my houses who obviously smokes," she said dismissively and carefully picked the faded filters from the sink.

"Who is it, Mom? Who has been breaking into your houses?" he continued to press.

"Please go get the mop and cleaning kit from my car. Don't forget the candle. I want to be ready for this afternoon."

"Dammit, Mom! Why won't you admit to me that Mark was here?" he finally exploded. Clara tried to give him the "Mom" eyes for his language, but they had no effect.

"Mark doesn't smoke, so it couldn't have been him," she tried weakly.

"Trevor does."

"It's only been a few houses," she said slowly. "It was a couple weeks ago." Clara leaned against the counter still refusing to look at her son.

"Why didn't you say anything? Did you tell the police at least?"

"No. What would have been the use? It showed where he had been, not where he is. I don't see how that could help at all."

"Still, it's something. It says that Mark is basically living on the street. He still might be, or worse."

"I know." She sighed.

"You know, but you don't care." Isaac finally said it, the words that he had been afraid to utter until now.

Her red-rimmed eyes finally met his, hurt and pain in them. "You think I don't care? My son is out there. A child on the streets, so of course I care. It's just…"

"What? That he's gay so you can't be bothered to look for him?" he said.

"Your father and I have spent weeks looking for him. You have no right to say that we haven't."

"I've been watching you. You've been half-assing it. The only time either one of you actually go out to look for him is when I make you. Nobody has replaced the flyers around town, either. You guys haven't even talked to the Buells since I've been back home. What am I supposed to think?" Isaac honed in.

"I don't want Mark on the street. I want him safe."

"But do you want him back home?" When she didn't answer, he asked again. "Mom, do you want Mark to come back home?"

Clara grimaced, and a hand went to her swollen belly. For a moment he thought she might be faking it to get out of answering, but as she clutched the counter, he could tell that it was real.

"I think we should go. It might be time," she said, taking a deep breath.

"Let me help you," he said, taking her arm and helping her to the car. He may not have gotten her to admit it, but now he knew the truth. He might have find his brother himself.

XVII.

"We can't just stay here all the time," Mark said. "We've already mended the fences and cleaned up the pasture. Now what?"

"If you're bored, I've got something that will keep you busy." Trevor pointed at his crotch.

Mark chose to ignore it. He picked up a threadbare copy of an old Fredrick Pohl novel, something about medieval knights hitching a ride on a spaceship. He needed a touch of the slightly ridiculous right now. He had attempted to read more of *Dahlgren*, but there were too many uncomfortable parallels for him to enjoy it.

"I'm serious. One of us needs to get a job. I don't want to stay here for much longer. The heater makes me nauseous. This isn't a way to live. This is temporary."

"I know. We just need to wait it out. Things will look up."

"You keep saying that. We're almost out of money, the winter is getting colder, and we're running out of options." Mark could see from the look on his friend's face that reasoning with him wasn't going to work. Trevor's bloodshot eyes betrayed the fact that he still had some leftover marijuana stashed. It only served to increase Mark's anger and desolation.

"But this is great. Don't you see? It's like we're living off the land. We have just what we need and nothing more. Best of all is the freedom. No parents to tell us what to do, no school to try and institutionalize us, and no God to point his finger at us and judge." Trevor stood up and reveled in his triumph.

Mark had to admit, he enjoyed the flavor of freedom, but the isolation chilled his bones more than the air outside did. He agreed that God wasn't pointing fingers. Not in the way that Trevor meant it. From realization that can only come from rock bottom, he knew that God wasn't some judgmental prick. God was hope. It was the only thing that made sense to him since they had walked into this decaying house. God was hope, and there was no hope there; ergo there was no God for them. He had no family he could turn to. They lived in the heart of Mormon country where entire towns, Grason and Cache especially, were run by the "moral" majority. As long as they were here, they had no hope. As long as they were a couple of broke kids with no resources, they weren't going anywhere.

Mark understood why Trevor had tried to stay high so much. It was his escape from a world on the constant verge of chewing him up and spitting him out. Mark's had always been his dreams, his fantasy worlds. Whether buried in a novel or dreaming about a future building for the stars, he had used that for his escape. Now he didn't even have that. He packed some books and forgot to bring his future along with him. He felt sure that there was no way any advanced engineering program would pick him up now. He was officially a dropout. Instead of keeping his mouth shut and head down, he let himself get spit out. It would have been easy to blame Trevor. He'd instigated the entire process. But Mark didn't have the energy for it. He was finding a new best friend more insidious and infectious than Trevor could ever be. It was apathy.

"Let's walk into town," Trevor said boisterously.

"Why?"

"You're right, for once. We need money. I figure if we each take a street corner, I'm sure we can turn enough tricks to afford dinner tonight."

"Sometimes it's hard to tell if you're kidding or not." Mark stood up and stretched. If nothing else, maybe the walk would cure his restlessness in both mind and body.

"I'm sure there are bound to be a few help wanted signs up. Let's go."

They exited into the pale sunlight. Last night's dusting of snow still clung to the shadows while the rest of it had disappeared. As they passed the main house they could see the old man standing on his covered porch. His crutch under his arm and a bottle in his hand, he just glared at the boys as they walked past.

"That guy needs laid," Trevor said when they reached the road.

"Be my guest," Mark mumbled. The less he thought of their "landlord," the better.

The boys talked little on the couple miles into town. The wind couldn't decide if it wanted to blow or not, so it intermittently bit at their faces.

Cache only had a one main street and a small number of side streets with shop fronts and businesses that might have a help wanted sign in the window. In less than an hour, they had walked past every shop. Either no one was hiring or the building was empty.

"We could go out to the junkyard and try to get jobs taking apart cars," Trevor suggested.

"That's ten miles the opposite direction. How are we going to get to work each day?" Mark said, hoping that he wasn't serious about it.

"Good point. I'm going back to the gas station we passed and see if I can bum a smoke from someone," Trevor said.

He walked forward with sudden purpose as Mark stood where he was. He felt painfully exposed and washed over with a need to get off the street. He walked into a second hand store.

The dusty linoleum floor and faded paint on the walls seemed to fit his spirit. The mix and match collection of worn racks and shelving held discarded and forgotten knick-knacks. He pretended to look through stubby racks of worn and almost tattered clothes. *I belong here*, he thought. *With all this stuff that's used and no longer wanted. I should just sit on a shelf and wait out the years here with a faded twenty-five cent sticker on my forehead.*

As he wandered, the stumpy woman who loomed behind the counter watched him. She wore a faded smock with the name Sheila embroidered on it. He wanted to tell her that there wasn't anything worth shoplifting so she could relax, but he kept his tongue instead. Unable to take her scrutiny any longer he decided to leave.

"You look hungry," she said from over the counter. Her voice betrayed too many cigarettes, and her face red from a life in the weather.

Mark wasn't sure how to respond to that. He was hungry. Only eating once a day to conserve their dwindling cash had an effect on his stomach. He wasn't ready to admit to anything at this point, though, even to a complete stranger.

"I'm a teenager. I'm always hungry," he said with a wan smile.

"I'm sure that's true, but you look like you've missed a few meals lately. I can hook you up with a couple meal vouchers for Eddy's next door. The food is good," she said.

Mark hesitated for only a second before approaching her. They could use a hot meal. He was getting sick of subsisting on gas station food.

"Yeah, it's been a few days since we've had anything that was actual food," he admitted as she dug out two rectangular slips of paper from a drawer. She scribbled an initial on the bottom and handed them over.

"Will two be enough?" she asked.

"Yeah, it's just the two of us," Mark said hastily.

"I don't mean to be nosy, but what about your parents? They on hard times?"

"Uh, yeah. It's been tight lately. My brother and I can use these. It would help my parents out on the food bill," he said, trying to think quickly. He held his breath hoping that she bought it.

"It's been going around since the dairies started having troubles. This damn drought has been killing us. Hopefully we get some *real* snowfall this year." She clucked. "My nephew was let go at the big Roscoe dairy, and now he and his wife are in debt up to their ears."

"Like you said, it's been going around. Thanks," he said, turning to go. He needed to find Trevor and cash these in before Sheila changed her mind.

"Hold on," she called, and he stopped in his tracks. *Here we go*, he thought. *She's not buying any of it.* "Something just occurred to me. I've been looking for a kid like you."

"Um, why is that?" If she knew he was a runaway, then there would be cops, and he would wind up back home. And all they would do was kick him out as soon as the cops left. Then he truly would have nowhere to go.

"This place ain't much, but it does get kinda dirty. All I have is myself and the occasional volunteer to keep the place up. I can't give you much, but if you want to come in once a week to sweep and dust, maybe a few other little odds and ends, I'll pay you twenty bucks a week."

"That would be awesome." Mark immediately perked up. "Anything you need, I'll be willing to do."

"I can tell you're a good kid, and I feel sorry for the families that are struggling right now. Lord knows, I'm one of them. Can you come in Fridays after school?" she asked, and he nodded emphatically. "Good. I probably should get the okay from your parents, though. This is all under the table, but still, you are a minor."

"No. That's probably not a good idea. My parents keep telling me that I can't get a job after school because they think it will affect my grades. My grades are good, and I really want to help out. Can we just keep this between us for now?" Mark said with only the minutest twinge of guilt for lying. She examined him for a moment before answering.

"Sure, I understand. Parents can be that way sometimes. It'll be just between us."

Mark thanked her again, promising to be there Friday afternoon. Just as he pushed open the door, she wished him a good Thanksgiving. It surprised him that it was already the holiday season. He hadn't even noticed. Focusing on the potential of money instead of giving into the weight of depression, he hurried on. Those twenty dollars could keep them in kerosene and Raman noodles. His stomach rumbled as he fingered the food vouchers in his pocket. The sooner he could get Trevor, the better.

XVIII.

Through the windows, the world shone like a bright white mass as Mark carefully swept between the shelving of out-of-date baubles. He had cleaned the back bathroom and dusted all the shelves. The only thing left was to sweep. Sheila had her head buried in a supermarket tabloid. The small bell above the door tinkled, and he looked up to see two teenage girls walk in. Paying them no attention, he continued his sweeping. They quietly tittered and mumbled amongst themselves. As they walked past him, he noticed Sheila keeping an eye on them. Surreptitiously, she glanced at Mark. After a moment, he realized that the girls were probably the same age as him, meaning that technically they should be classmates.

They stopped to look at a couple of chipped and creepy-looking porcelain dolls. Mark started sweeping toward them and said a quiet hello. He tried to make it sound as if it were just distant classmates passing by. They both looked up at him and after a pause said hello back. Hoping it was enough to fool Sheila, he continued on with his task. Catching a glance at the girls again he noted that they looked close enough to be sisters. Maybe they were.

Noticing his gaze, they began quietly talking in Spanish. They were both dark and pretty, he noted. Seized with a sudden need to make friends, he wanted to go over and talk to them. He'd felt like a fugitive ever since they came to town, and fugitives didn't make friends. They both looked up at him again, the taller one giving him wide smile. There was something different about her that he couldn't put his finger on.

He dumped the pile of dirt he had accumulated in the trash bin and returned the broom to the back room. Without looking at the girls, he made a straight line to Sheila at the counter. He didn't need her to know that he didn't go to school with these two. As far as she was concerned, he was just a high school student needing some extra cash, not a runaway queer barely surviving.

"Thanks again," she said putting the money in his hand. "You worked your ass off for this. Just wait until you get a real job." She cackled. He politely laughed with her and left.

The snow had slowed down to fat and lazy flakes. He wasn't looking forward to walking through the ankle-deep drifts in just his sneakers. The layers of socks would only keep his feet dry for so long.

He hadn't even made it to the corner when heard someone behind him call out. "Hey!" the two girls were walking up to him. "You're new in town, right?"

"Um, yeah," he said nervously.

"I thought so. Haven't seen you at school," the taller one said with a hint of an accent. Her hood was up, but her face was still visible.

"I don't go to school, um, here."

"Fabiana," the shorter one introduced herself, brushing her long, dark hair away from her large brown eyes. "And this is Ernesto."

"Stop calling me that." The other girl's voice dropped an octave. "I'm Angela." Suddenly Mark realized the difference he couldn't spot earlier. Underneath the make-up was a subtle hint of stubble. She noticed his scrutiny and nervously looked around.

"I am not calling you Angela. Every Angela we know is a puta," Fabiana scolded her sister. "I still prefer Anissa."

"Hi, I'm...Anissa, then." She said her voice going back up to her previous register.

"I'm Mark. And I like Anissa better too. Angela does sound like a...puta name." As he said it, his face grew red, and both girls laughed hard. Nervously rubbing the back of his neck, Mark took a step back. His sudden need to make friends had receded. He just wanted to get home where no one knew he was just a discarded youth. "It was really nice to meet you both, but I probably should get home."

"Where do you live? we can walk with you. We're bored, and it's nice to actually meet someone for once. In a town like this, it's always the same faces," Fabiana said.

"Well, it's out a few miles from town," Mark started to stammer.

"And it is a palace," a familiar voice said from behind. Trevor walked up and put an arm around Mark's neck, pulling him close. "I'm Trevor. I see you've met my man Mark."

"Told you," Anissa told her sister. They introduced themselves to Trevor.

"I just came down to walk you home." Trevor held Mark uncomfortably close, something that he had never done before. He peered at Anissa for a moment then asked, "Tranny?" Mark rolled his eyes and broke Trevor's grip.

"Sorry, he has no concept of subtlety or politeness," Mark apologized.

"I don't mean it to be bad. I'm just asking a question. To be honest, with a closer shave, no one would be able to tell," Trevor said.

"I am. I'll take it as a compliment instead of hating you," Anissa said, raising an eyebrow. "This time."

"Don't say 'tranny,'" Fabiana corrected. "It's 'transgender,' or you could just try 'person.'" Anissa gave her sister a look that held both embarrassment and gratitude.

Trevor put his hands up, "My apologies. Honestly, I didn't know."

"Well, we should go." Mark said, not wishing to chance Trevor embarrassing him anymore than he already had.

"I don't suppose you two know where a guy can get some green, do you?" Trevor asked, suddenly conspiratorial.

"I was actually hoping you had some." Fabiana laughed.

"Damn. Tell you what, if I find some, I'll let you know. If you find some, you let me know," he offered.

"Deal." She smiled.

They parted ways. The boys headed back to their home, and the girls went the opposite direction.

After a few minutes Trevor mused aloud, "You know, Anissa makes a pretty passable girl. Kinda cute, if you're into that sort of thing." Mark mumbled an agreement. Trevor, excited at meeting new people, was too hyper to let it pass. "You into that sort of thing?"

"What sort of thing?" Mark asked even though he knew better.

"Girls. Even ones that aren't quite girls." Trevor playfully nudged him.

"I think Ernesto sees herself as a woman. If that's the case, why shouldn't I? She's Angela, or Anissa, or whomever she wants to be. People aren't always what you think they are. Sometimes they stray beyond the boundaries of what we think is normal. Nothing wrong with it."

"Jesus, I didn't mean for you to get all philosophical. I was giving you shit because of the eyes you were giving Fabiana." Trevor rolled his eyes.

"I was not giving her 'eyes,'" Mark defended himself. *Who am I convincing, Trevor or myself?* he worried. He didn't think he was staring at the girls, but they were attractive. Was that wrong of him?

"You aren't joining the other side, are you?" Trevor continued to tease.

"No, I'm not joining any sides." He tried join in the fun, but instead he came out sounding annoyed. "I'm the same as always."

"Worse yet, you go both ways. Dear god, no! When we get home, I'm staging an intervention to bring you back to where you belong. Choose a side, dear. Choose a side!"

Trevor's mocking, regardless of how inappropriate, usually made him laugh. This time he only smiled politely. Sometimes things were said simply because he thought it was funny, but sometimes not. Trevor seemed in a good mood, and Mark didn't want to be a wet blanket for once.

He took a serious breath and then looked Trevor in the eye. "I am bi, and the reason I know is because I did your mom. Twice." Even though he meant it to sound like a joke, a mote of excited relief briefly flared. The relief mixed with a new sensation of realization: *I am bisexual.* The thought rang clear and true in his head and in his heart. Something heavy slid off of him. If he knew nothing in his life to be true, this one fact he could always keep.

Trevor's laughter cut the sweet feeling of revelation short. "I'm pretty sure that would actually make you gayer. Knowing my dad, he took one look at me then decided not to chance another one. My mom probably hasn't gotten any in sixteen years."

"That's...disturbing." Mark grimaced.

He thought about his parents and his little sister. Was she born yet? He wondered what would happen when she came into the world without him there. Cold realization crawled over him that he might not ever meet her. Or if he did it would be such a far shot into the future that he would be nothing more than a long-lost relative. A face to recognize only from stories other family members told of him. He shook the thought away. The less he thought of his family the better. Therein lay too much pain.

XlX

Mark knew the twenty dollar wage in his pocket wasn't going to get them much. There was only so much Raman and sugarless Kool-aid they could consume. They needed some real food. Standing in the aisle and facing the canned goods, Mark grabbed a can of corn and looked at it.

"You see anybody around?" Mark asked Trevor without looking up.

"No." Trevor said with a casual glance up the aisle. Mark carefully slipped the can into his coat pocket. By the time they reached the end, Mark had stashed beans, carrots, and rice.

"I still think I should be the one with the contraband," Trevor mumbled. He had lifted before, just a few candy bars and magazines, but he feared that normally straight-laced Mark would bungle it up.

"Just go and pay for the Raman and bread. And don't forget the sugar. I can't handle bland Kool-aid anymore," Mark said, slouching to hide the odd lumps in his coat. They walked to the front of the store. A bored clerk stood at the cash register watching them. "Here, you pay for it. I'm going outside for a smoke,"

Mark said loudly as she slapped the twenty into Trevor's hand. He shuffled out the door, trying to look as bored and unconcerned with life as possible.

A long minute passed as he leaned against a white-washed cinderblock wall. He held his breath until Trevor emerged, swinging the bag at his side. "I'm proud of you. There's a criminal in your heart, just waiting to get out."

"Yeah, well, we need to eat," Mark said.

The trek home was long and quiet. By the time they walked through their front door, the shadows had grown long. Mark emptied his pockets onto the counter and began fixing their dinner. Trevor pulled a steak from the shopping bag.

"I saw you eyeballing this, so I stuffed it down my pants," he said, handing it to Mark.

"Always pulling your meat out of your pants and giving it to someone," he said, taking the steak.

"I'll only give it to you." Trevor touched Mark's arm then disappeared into the shadow darkened living room.

Neither one of them was comfortable with these little moments of intimacy, but they had begun to pop up more frequently. He had no idea what they were anymore: friends, lovers, or roommates. Clinging together for warmth and security was one thing, but something else grew between them that neither spoke about. They had physical moments, but they were spontaneous and sporadic. Mark didn't want to dwell on it much. It was what it was.

He connected the small green propane cylinder to the camp stove. It felt light, and he hoped he could at least cook tonight's meal. They weren't very big, but he wondered if they could walk out with at least one without a backpack. A future worry, he decided. They might have to deal with cold canned vegetables until he got paid again from the second-hand store.

"Here, clean this." He handed Trevor a cheap frying pan.

"Why do I have to do the dishes all the time?" he whined.

"I don't know if we have enough to actually consider them in plural."

"Why do I have to do the *dish* all the time?" Trevor grinned.

"Because you make me do all the cooking, and I found mouse shit in that," Mark mock scolded.

"You'll make someone a great wife someday."
Trevor laughed as he walked outside to the water
spigot.

"Blow me."

***

The sweet tangy smell of marijuana clung to the
air. Trevor sprawled across the sleeping bags in the
bedroom while Fabiana and Ernesto sat next to each
other, leaning against the wall. Their friend, a sandy
haired teen named Ryan, sat by them. Mark sat on the
floor against the far wall and faced them all. They
giggled and talked, though Mark wasn't paying a lot of
attention. He was high, and mellow for once. It was a
wonderful feeling; he had forgotten what it was like to
not be tense and scared every waking moment.

The two Latina siblings were true to their word,
and once they scored a bag, they had Ryan drive them
over. Mark waited for their surly and disgusting
"landlord" to come pitch a bitch because they had
guests, but he had so far not shown. Mark suspected
the guy was more bark than bite.

"I'm surprised that you didn't come over as Anissa," Mark said to Ernesto. After he said he it occurred to him that maybe their friend didn't know.

"To be honest, I've only gone public with Anissa that once," he said, taking a small metal pipe from his sister. "I was scared to death the entire time. It's not like this piece of shit town is the most open-minded. You are one of the few who has accepted me as who I am." Mark's cheeks went rosy for a moment.

"This town sucks. In junior high I got the snot beat out of me by a bunch of jocks because it got out that I was gay," Ryan said as he stared at the ceiling. "The funny thing is, I'm pretty sure one of them is dating a lesbian right now."

"I don't suppose her name is Lindsey," Trevor said off-handedly.

"Yeah, she's new. How did you know?" Ryan sat up and faced Trevor. He leaned in a little closer than Mark was comfortable with.

"We knew her from Grason. We went to school together," Mark quickly interjected.

"...and church, and our parents hung out together. She was the scandal of the town for a while,"

Trevor said, not taking his eyes off the boy. "We really should go say hi to her."

"I wouldn't," Fabiana said. "She's doing everything she can to pretend to be straight. She isn't fooling anyone, though. We all know what happened at her last school. I've seen her checking me out." She giggled.

"Why shouldn't she? I'd check you out too." Mark joked.

"Why must I always be surrounded by maricones?" she sighed in mock exasperation.

"Because my milkshake brings all the boys to the yard." Ernesto said, and they all laughed.

"So what's the deal with you being transgendered?" Trevor enunciated the word for effect. "Or do you just like dressing up in women's clothes?" Mark winced.

"I am all woman. I've always felt a little off, like something was different for me. I mean, I'm sure everyone in this room has felt that way. In this straight-dominated world, it's inevitable. But for me it was different. It wasn't just that I liked boys. In fact, that came later. It just felt that I was not quite right in my own body. Like I was wearing someone else's skin.

The first time I can remember seeing Fabiana in a Sunday dress, I wanted to be her. It was more than just wanting to wear a dress. It was wanting to be just like her. Sure, I wanted to be pretty like her, but it wasn't until later that I understood it better. I wanted to live as comfortable in my skin as she did in hers. As I got older, I did my best to try and forget it, but I couldn't. It always loomed there in the back of my head. Somehow I didn't fit with myself. It got worse when puberty came. I hated it. I didn't ask for all these changes to my body and wished they would all go away."

"He was an insufferable bitch," his sister laughed, but gently. Mark could see a fierce need to protect her older sibling in the girl. He admired it and wondered if his own brother had ever felt the same.

"I still am," Ernesto replied. "Becoming a girl is always something I have to do in my head or when no one is home. When we met, it was the first, and so far only, time I ever went out in public as the real me. My parents can't find out. They wouldn't understand. But despite the fear, it felt liberating. I actually felt like myself for once."

187

"I'm glad I got a chance to meet the real you then," Mark said.

"So am I." Ernesto's gaze lingered on him.

"So no one else knows?" Trevor asked.

"No. Not yet. I still get teased and bullied from people, though."

"Yeah," Fabiana cut in, "and if that pendejo from your English class pushes you around one more time, I'm going to beat his ass."

"That guy has a screw loose," Ryan said. "I'd be careful with him."

Mark asked what they meant, and the three of them described a local kid they went to school with named Daniel. Daniel's streak of intolerance ran wide and deep. He came from a long line of white redneck stock. If you weren't a straight, white male and believed in the Lord Almighty (or at least his version), then you were scum and he wasted no time letting you know. He would often target the Mexican migrant community for his teases and slurs. Fabiana and Ernesto seemed to take a lot of the verbal abuse because they were often stuck with him in school.

"I act as straight as I can, but he just seems to know. Nasty taunts and dirty jokes at my expense were usually what I got when we were younger." Ernesto sighed.

"He tried to instigate a fight a couple weeks ago," Fabiana said. "The guy is a menace."

"Bring him on over here," Mark suggested. "We can bury him in the back yard." He pointed over his shoulder at the acres and acres of farmland. They all laughed at the joke.

"If you want to go by Angela, you can," Fabiana said, apologizing unprompted. "The other day I was just giving you shit."

"No, you were right. All the Angela's we know are putas. And besides, as Angela I was scared and confused. I'm not anymore. Anissa is a strong and liberated woman. That's who I am."

"Then in this house," Trevor announced loudly, "the name Ernesto is banned. Anyone who uses it will be flogged. And not in the fun way. Only the name Anissa will be used, for that is who you are." They all whooped in agreement.

As they all continued to talk and laugh, Mark felt his stomach grumble. He hadn't eaten today, and the bowl of noodles he had yesterday did little to dent the previous day's hunger. All they had left were noodles and a can of peas to eat. He craved real food so much it drove him crazy.

"I'm frickin' hungry," he said out loud without realizing it.

"Me too," Trevor said, but he was looking at Ryan while he said it. "I would give anything for some food right now."

"We could order a pizza," Fabiana offered. "Anyone have any money?" After a chorus of nos, she swore. "Damn. Now I want pizza."

"We could sell some of this for pizza money," Ryan pulled out a baggy from his pocket. "I spent all I had on this. I'm willing to part with it for the sake of hunger."

"How about we sell it to the meth-head that works down at the gas station?" Trevor suggested. They frequented the little convenience store a lot, and during the evening shift, a scabby, rail thin woman worked the counter. She looked fifty but they guessed that she was probably in her mid-thirties.

Trevor tried to sit up but then immediately lay back down. "Nope, too high."

"I'll go." Mark stood up. The gentle wave of calm he was riding had given him a confident apathy.

Ryan pinched off a corner of the plastic baggy and picked through the green.

"Here. It's mostly seeds and stems, but she won't know it until afterwards."

Mark took it and stuffed into his coat pocket. It was more than hunger that motivated him to leave. He hated the subtle flirting between Ryan and Trevor. He couldn't handle it much longer.

As he got to the door he called out, "Someone order the pizza, and I'll be back with the money."

"What's the address here?" Fabiana asked.

"Middle of nowhere at the corner of hopeless and desperate," he answered back, and they all laughed. He meant it to be funny, but it didn't feel funny.

XX.

The Jensen house had hit maximum occupancy. Caryn meandered into the living room where her sister held court. All the wives had gathered around her and baby Rachel, cooing and smiling. Her brother-in-law had the husbands clustered in the kitchen, talking crops and cars. The small children who had come with their parents were scattered about with their faces buried in some sort of flashing device. Isaac leaned against counter in the kitchen, deciding that he would just stay near the food. Caryn looked around for Trevor's parents. Sandy was clustered with the women while Aaron leaned against a far wall, a plastic cup of punch clutched in his hand. His tall, gray and gaunt frame was tense, like that of a snake about to strike. He made little attempt to disguise his lack of enthusiasm about being there or being anywhere near this family. She couldn't fathom what sort of man could be so angry at all times. He wore it like a comfortable suit, a stark contrast to his wife's bubbly public persona.

In a time now long gone, Caryn and Sandy had once been close friends. Now they simply lived in the same town, each pretending to greet each other as old acquaintances would when they happened upon one another. Sandy wasn't the person she once was; now she was docile and wore the mask of being happy in a sad sort of way. Her functions in the church were her only social events. Church was the only time anyone saw her husband, save for his job managing a combining and thrashing business with his brother.

Caryn fought hard to hold her tongue. She had wanted to get her family and Trevor's family together and talk about the missing boys but so far lacked the impetus to do it. Now that they were in the same house, she felt almost obligated. Those boys were out there, and she couldn't shake the feeling that they hadn't gone far. In Idaho, you either stayed close by or got as far away as you could. Some speculation claimed that they ran off to San Francisco or maybe Portland, but she suspected that people were just coming up with places they perceived to be generically gay. She had to find them before they did manage to get that far away. Maybe living with their families wasn't the answer; she could concede that. But they were still too young to be trying to survive on their own.

Isaac came up beside her. "It seems so strange to have a baby sister. It's always just been Mark and me. Now that Rachel is here, things seem so different." He looked at the sleeping blonde bundle in his mother's arms. "I wish Mark were here."

"Me too. I would give anything to know where he was so I could bring him back," Caryn said.

"What if we did know where he was and found him, but he didn't want to come back? It seems like we've been talking like he just needs to be found, and then everything will be all right." He had been keeping that fear to himself. He could admit it to his aunt, given her similar attitude.

"That scares me even more than not finding him. But we'll cross that bridge when we come to it." Truth be told, that idea scared her worse than not being able to find him. It would only compound helplessness on top of more helplessness, a feeling she was beginning to hate.

"I noticed you keep looking at the Buells'. Please tell me you're not going to confront them." He had seen the look in his aunt's eye, and it was what prompted him to come up to her in the first place.

"I'm trying not to. It's just… they gave up so soon. It was like they did whatever your parents organized out of obligation. It bothers me that they aren't bothered that their only child is out there."

"I think they are more bothered about what their son is than where he is," Isaac said grimly and drained his cup of punch.

He went back in the kitchen to refill his glass and passed by LaVell, who bragged to the group of men about his son's tenure at BYU, obviously ignoring the fact that Isaac wasn't there right now like he was supposed to be. Grabbing a few celery sticks and dipping them liberally in a cup of ranch dressing, Isaac decided that he needed to get away from the group for a bit. Especially if Aunt Caryn decided she wanted a confrontation. He knew that if it came down to it, he would back her before his own parents.

He walked down the hallway toward his room when one of the young children came zooming from Mark's room holding a model rocket and making whooshing noises. Inside two more kids poked around.

"Hey! Get out of there." He barked at them and they scurried off. Isaac came up behind the blond-haired little boy who had taken the rocket and snatched it out of his hand. "This isn't yours. You stay out of my brother's room. You have no right to go in there."

The room had gone quiet, but Isaac was too irritated to care. As he stalked back to shut the bedroom door, Aaron Buell said in a deep voice, "Careful youngster, you might catch the queer."

The young boy who had taken the rocket looked up at the tall man, then at his hand that had held the toy. LaVell called out from the kitchen as his wife covered up the sleeping baby in her arms with a blanket. Isaac spun on his heel, but Caryn got to the man first.

"You owe that child, my sister, and our family an apology." Caryn looked up at him, her own anger matching his own.

"I don't owe anyone a damned thing," he said quietly.

"Aaron..." Sandy said from a far corner, the fear in her eyes obvious. "Please don't."

"Your son is out there, as is my nephew, cold and scared. Maybe they aren't straight, maybe they are 'queer,' but they are still ours to care for and love."

"Caryn, don't do this," Clara said from the couch.

Caryn stood unfazed, though. Knowing her sister all too well, Clara looked to her husband to step in before things could possibly get worse. Instead,

LaVell just stood there, ready to step in only if things got physical. The abuse in the Buell household was known but unspoken of.

"I think it's that sort of archaic thinking that's put them out in the first place. Those boys…"

"What those boys are is no mistake. They are sinners. I won't put up with that," Aaron growled.

"It's only a sin if they act on it. You know that as well as I do." Caryn continued to challenge him.

"If they are out there on their own, they are now beyond the gaze of the Heavenly Father. Or so they think. They've sinned already. And if they ran off together, then they sinned long before that." Aaron's tone was venomous.

"You son of a bitch!" Anger crackled around Isaac. Caryn put a hand on his chest to stop him. He was surprised by her strength.

"I suggest you leave," LaVell said, taking a step forward. "I won't have this sort of talk in my house. Not with children present and especially in front of my daughter."

"C'mon, Sandy," Aaron said, but she was too busy dabbing her eyes with a Kleenex to pay attention. He grunted and left without her.

As the door slammed, she stood up and ran to the bathroom. One of the other women followed. Clara sat there, an undefined dark stare leveled at her sister.

"Son, why don't you check the freezer in the garage. See if we have anymore frozen punch," LaVell said. Isaac stomped off, still seething with anger.

"I'll go help him," Caryn said, no longer wanting to be in the room any more.

"No. You've helped plenty," Clara said. Carefully she stood. "I'm going to put Rachel to bed."

As she left, the guests looked around, made uncomfortable by what they had seen. LaVell looked at his sister-in-law and then looked away. Caryn realized that in that moment he stood a man at war with himself. What she had marked as reluctance to act was actually inner turmoil. Maybe he didn't toe the line that his wife drew after all. Deflated, she wanted to leave. She couldn't fix a situation she had only made worse. Quietly she went to gather her coat and saw Sandy emerge from the bathroom, puffy-eyed.

"Sandy, listen. I'm sorry," Caryn tried to apologize. "Let me take you home. It's the least I could do."

"Yeah, okay," she agreed after a small pause. "But only because I've been dying to ride in your sports car." A sad little smile escaped her lips. With a few half-hearted goodbyes, the women left the house and walked up to Caryn's small car. "Take the long way. It will give Aaron a few extra minutes to cool down."

They rode in silence. Caryn took a few wrong turns at Sandy's request. Staring out the window, Sandy said, "I pray for him. I pray for us all."

"I'm sure he's okay. Trevor is a smart kid, as is Mark." She said as reassuring as possible.

"You're right. He is, but it's his affliction that I pray about. It scares me to think what he might be doing out there just to survive."

"This is southern Idaho, not the streets of Hollywood. I seriously doubt he's had to resort to hustling."

"I hope not. But there are so many temptations out there for him," Sandy said.

They were quiet for another moment before Caryn said, "I'm just saying I don't understand what all the castigation is about. I remember a party back when we were in college..."

"Caryn, stop. I know what you're going to say, and it's nothing like this," Sandy said.

"If you want to tell yourself that she kissed you, then go ahead. But I was there, and what I saw was something completely different. You kissed her like you meant it."

"That was completely different. And there was a lot of alcohol at those parties. It was nothing."

"You two were making out for a long time. I think the only reason you stopped was because Rodney Tipton came and threw you over his shoulder and disappeared with you for the rest of the night."

"I am not a hypocrite," Sandy said.

"I didn't say you were."

"You implied it," Sandy accused. Caryn just stared at the road. "There was a lot of alcohol. That's why in the Bible says that alcohol is bad. I know Trevor drinks. It's probably the same for him."

"Good thing it doesn't say anything in the Bible about prescription medicines," Caryn muttered.

"Stop this goddamn car," Sandy growled.

"I'm sorry. That was out of line. I'm really sorry. I'm just stressed out. Let me take you home. I know that you aren't gay, and I wasn't implying that.

I'm saying that the human experience is a lot more than what we think it is. Sometimes we say that something is harmful, but really it's just people being honest."

"I wish I could agree with that."

They pulled up to the Buell residence. Wordlessly, Sandy got out and quickly walked into the house. Caryn watched the door close behind her and took a breath. Things were only going to get worse before they got better, and she hated it.

***

"So how are your grades? Working here isn't hurting them, is it?" Sheila asked as Mark swept between two racks of faded children's clothes.

"They're good. No problems there," he said, but her scrutiny made him feel uncomfortable.

"You're a junior this year, right? My sister's kid is too. You might have a class together," she said pointedly.

Mark didn't like where this was going, so he just kept his head down and swept. "Maybe."

"Mark, I don't like liars. You're a good kid, but I can tell you've been feeding me a line of bull. You don't go to school in Cache, do you? You drop out?"

He stopped sweeping and sighed. It was useless to lie now. "I don't go to school in Cache. I'm not even from here. I ran away from home."

"I know." She pulled out two crisp sheets of paper from under the register. Flattening them on the counter, Mark recognized what they were immediately. One had his picture; the other had Trevor's. They were school pictures taken last year, with big red letters above that screamed "Missing."

"I found these at the post office. I take it your parents don't know you're here?" She sat back on her stool.

"No. They don't know where I am. I'm not even sure they care."

"That can't be true. They're your parents. They have to care."

"If they did, I wouldn't have run away. It felt pretty apparent that I wasn't welcome anymore."

"I'm real sorry to hear that. I'm also sorry to hear that you chose Cache to run away to. Why the hell did you choose this crap hole?" Sheila shook her head.

It did seem like an absurd notion to run away to an even worse place than he'd left.

"Trevor has a cousin here, but he managed to get us kicked out." Mark said.

"Your 'brother,' I assume. Listen, I'm not one to judge. I kinda guessed you were flying a rainbow flag, but it don't matter to me. But we do have a problem." Mark knew what was coming. He leaned the broom up against the counter as she hit the no sale button on the cash register. "Now that I know you are a runaway, I have to let the authorities know. "

"No!" Mark's eyes got wide. "Please, no. It's just…they were abusive. I didn't feel safe there. Trevor's parents were the same. That's why we decided to leave together. If you have to call the cops, please give us a head start. We can't go back there." Lies flowed as quickly from his mouth. Guilt came rushing from behind it, but he swallowed it down. There was no way he was being forced back to an unbearable situation.

"If it's not safe, then I can understand why you don't want to go back." She crumpled up the posters and threw them in the trash. "I can't let you work here. It's nothing personal, but I have to watch my own

203

back." She pulled four twenties from the tray and slid them towards him.

"What's this?"

"Catch a bus back home. Or if you can't do that, then just get the hell out of here."

Mark took the money from her and put it in his pocket. With nothing to say he left. The evening chased him home, its familiar chill seeping in. With the chill, despair began to slowly wrap around him. They were just barely surviving on what little he was making. The eighty dollars in his pocket would only last for so long.

Mark thought about what Sheila said. They could catch a bus and just leave. It wouldn't be that hard to catch a ride to Grason and hop a bus. They could probably make it as far as Salt Lake City. If he could scrounge a little more, maybe he could make it as far as Seattle. They had only each other, he knew that, but it felt more and more like Trevor was only concerned with himself lately. Especially since they had met Fabiana's friend Ryan.

"Hey you," a familiar voice called out. He was so lost in his thoughts, he almost missed Fabiana walking toward him. "Off work?"

"Permanently," Mark said glumly.

"That sucks. I know what will make it better—food. My mom is making dinner tonight and I invited you and Trevor over."

Mark's initial reaction was to politely decline, but a home cooked meal sounded like a little piece of heaven. "That would be fantastic."

***

"Your mom seems nice," Mark said as they sat in Fabiana and Anissa's living room. Here Anissa had to be Ernesto, and Mark stayed mindful of the fact.

"Yeah, she likes to take in strays," Fabiana said. Mark was about to protest but then he looked at Trevor and them himself. They both burst out laughing. To say they looked like strays was putting it mildly. "But she doesn't know about my brother. Let's keep it butch up in here. As you can tell from the décor, it's all about the Jesus in this house." The pictures of Jesus Christ and the many crosses left little doubt of the Catholicism.

"It's cool. We both escaped from Mormon parents, so blending isn't a problem," Trevor said.

Ernesto walked into the small living room just behind his mother, Lupe. Ernesto had a small bruise on his brow. Mark suspected that there had been another run-in with the bully Daniel. He'd attempted to ask Fabiana about it right after they arrived, but she shut him down. When they were first invited to dinner, the boys were both a little nervous. Fabiana had warned them that his parents were "old school" in their belief. Their father, Julio, worked late and wouldn't be home for dinner.

"You boys are so skinny. Don't you ever eat?" Lupe turned to her daughter and said, "*Usan drogas?*"

"No mama, they aren't. They are into sports. Mark plays soccer," Fabiana reassured her.

"Good. Come eat," she said. They followed her into the dining room. Mark felt his stomach roil and churn at the amazing smells of hot, fresh food.

"You got lucky, she made *molé*," Fabiana said as she sat down.

"I don't know what that is, but I'll eat all of it," Trevor said, staring at the covered dish and the steaming tortilla warmer next to it.

Lupe sat down, and Trevor immediately grabbed his fork. Playfully, she slapped his hand and then took it, bowing her head.

"Going native already?" Mark whispered.

Trevor kicked him under the table. After Fabiana said a prayer in Spanish, Mark realized that he had said his own in English.

If heaven existed, both boys agreed, it was going to be filled with homemade tortillas, rice, and *molé*. Trevor took a bite of a tender bit of chicken, and the thick, brown sauce dribbled down his chin. Without thinking Mark grabbed his napkin to wipe it off for him, all the while making fun of him for being such a slob. Fabiana made a sound and gave them a disapproving look. Trevor quickly took the napkin and Mark went back to his own food.

With full and happy stomachs, the table had been cleared and the boys were about to leave. They both thanked the woman profusely for the meal.

"You boys, please be careful," she said and handed them a heavy shopping bag. Mark peeked in and saw that it was leftovers. "Your father will be home soon," she said to her daughter. Fabiana just nodded.

"Okay, time to go before you eat us out of house and home." She led them out of the house.

Once outside Mark turned to her. "Did we do something wrong?"

"No, my father will be home soon."

"I take it he doesn't take well to queers sneaking about his casa," Trevor said.

"He's old fashioned. I think he suspects something is up with his only son but pretends there isn't. It's hard to say what his reaction would be," she explained.

"Oh," was all he could say. They said their goodbyes and trudged homeward in the dark.

The warm fuzzy feeling he had from the hot meal was starting to wear off as the chill of the night mingled with a return to reality. Their lives were upside down, every day full of a heavy freedom. This freedom had a cost, he began to realize. He had been taught that freedom was the dispeller of all things bad, but this freedom they shared only traded one set of bad for another.

XXI.

When the boys returned to the house, they fired up the heater. The tang of burning kerosene filled the house, and Mark opened the window in the bedroom. Huddled together on the mattress they enjoyed the post meal glow. They didn't speak; instead they watched the shadows on the wall made from the small red glow of the old heater.

"How are we going to pay rent?" Mark said, breaking the silence. "We need to get another job going or your 'boyfriend' is going to kick us out."

"Maybe he has other jobs for us to do. And why is he my boyfriend?" Trevor asked.

"Because you two get along so well," Mark teased. "Might be just as well. This could be the time to leave."

"I like this place, though. It's starting to grow on me," Trevor said. "And besides, we can't leave. There's a chance we can have more of Fabiana and Anissa's food. Damn, that was good."

"It felt good to sit at a table and eat again," Mark said.

"I'm sure you thoroughly enjoyed the company," Trevor said. Mark felt a barb in the statement but was confused as to where it came from.

"They're good people," Mark said diplomatically.

"I've been wondering about you lately," Trevor said. "You've been acting strange." When Mark asked what he meant, Trevor just shrugged in the dark. After a moment, he said, "I've seen the way you've looked at Fabiana. Even Anissa, when she's dressed as a girl."

"Listen, getting a nice hot meal was practically orgasmic for me. I'm sure it was just foodgasms you were seeing," Mark said calmly.

Inside, his heart was thumping. If he had been looking at the girls any differently, he hadn't noticed. He hated to ruin a good night, but if Trevor was approaching the subject, then maybe it was time to have the talk. They had been dancing around the subject for weeks now. His frustration swelled because he couldn't be sure whether he could talk to his only friend about who he really was.

"No, it wasn't the food. It was Fabiana's dark eyes and batting eyelashes. You're into her."

The accusation, spiteful and ragged, couldn't be ignored. Mark reeled from the sudden hostility of it. If they were ever going to have the discussion tonight might as well be the night. "She wasn't batting her eyelashes," Mark said.

"No, but you were at her. It's pathetic." Trevor sat up on the mattress. "You've been lying to me and probably yourself. You just need to own up."

"Own up to what?" Mark sat up as well and faced his friend. "What is my crime, Trevor?"

"You think Fabiana is hot. Admit it."

Mark finally snapped. "Yes! Maybe I do find her attractive. Is that a problem?

"Man, whatever." Trevor rolled his eyes and turned away. Mark grabbed his shoulder and stopped him.

"No, we're going to talk about this. I do find her attractive. I'm not going to ask her out on any dates or anything, but she is cute. So what?" He felt pushed away and it was too much. First his parents and now his best friend.

"If you aren't gay, then why the hell did you tell your parents you were? You could be sleeping in your

warm bed. Did you just want to be part of the club?"
Trevor shot back.

"Club? What club? The Stuck In The Middle Of
Nowhere Freezing Your Ass Off Club? That's where all
the cool kids are? Jesus, Trevor, this isn't about being a
part of some group. It's about being able to be
ourselves. I'm not gay, and I'm not saying I'm straight
either."

"Then what the hell is left?" Trevor sneered.

"I'm bisexual."

"So now you're bi? Must make it easier then.
That will be your way out now. You can go back home
and go snuggle up with some chick, and you'll be fine."
The malice in Trevor's voice slapped Mark in the face.
He had never heard it come from him before, but Mark
had no intention of letting it derail him.

"If I'm having this argument with you, then
apparently it isn't making anything any easier," he
yelled back at him. "This isn't a realization that has
come easy to me. I didn't understand it for a long time,
and I still don't, not completely. But yes, I am
bisexual."

"Guys just aren't enough for you. Let's go back
over to the girls' house. Hell, you can have a

threesome with Anissa as well. That's gotta be a wet dream come true." Trevor stood up.

"I don't want to have sex with them. I can find a girl attractive without wanting to get in their pants, can't I?"

"Yes, you can, and that's called gay."

"It's like arguing in a circle with you." Mark huffed. All he wanted was a modicum of understanding.

"No, it's not. It's very clear. You're all stressed out and scared. I get it. I am too. But it's made you confused and looking for a way out of the problem. Being gay is what led you to this, so in your mind, if you were a fence sitter, then it would make things easier." Trevor had that look on his face that said he thought he said something quite smart. It only served to infuriate Mark more.

"Dammit, no! I was struggling with this before we even got kicked out of town." He paused to take a calming breath and try again. "Listen. I am attracted to both men and women. This is something that I've been dealing with for a while, and I could really use a friend right now."

"Don't worry about it. You can't be switch hitter because it doesn't exist." As soon as the words left Trevor's lips, Mark surged with a fiery lump of anger, betrayal, and isolation he had never experienced before.

"I open up and tell you something, and your answer to it is 'it doesn't exist'?" he yelled. Trevor opened his mouth to say something, but Mark cut him off. "I swear to Christ, if you say that I'm just confused again, I will punch you in the face. This is all new to me. I need a friend, not a naysayer."

"Ask Fabiana. You obviously want her." Trevor scoffed.

"No, I don't!" Mark exploded again. "You aren't listening! She's cute, but that doesn't mean I want to be with her either. It doesn't always have to be one or the other."

"Well, I can't be sure of what you want now. Until you pick one, how can I trust you?" Trevor turned for the door.

"Trevor," Mark called after him.

"Whatever," he said and disappeared into the night.

***

After Trevor left, Mark raged. Tears sprang to his eyes, and he stomped up and down the house in the dim light of the heater. Hours of raw emotion raged while Mark released all the years of frustration and fear. He had hidden the person he thought he was from his family while hiding the real person from himself. The balancing act he had been doing all this time turned out to be more difficult than he realized. He made the decision to fall off of the wire, but no net waited for him. Freefalling into the void only showed him what true emptiness felt like.

Unknown hours passed by, and Trevor still had not returned. Sitting cross-legged on the bed, Mark felt empty. His fists hurt from pounding the walls, his throat ragged from screaming and howling his heart out, and the floor littered with miscellaneous debris he had thrown around. The suppressed emotions of the past and the held fears of the present poured out from him like a broken hydrant. After the storm, a zen-like peace blanketed him. He now sat as an empty vessel, devoid of the past. He enjoyed it while he could.

Before long, first light colored the horizon. The empty feeling he had enjoyed began to fill with worry, then guilt. Trevor had been gone all night. Mark knew that he hadn't made Trevor leave, but if he had kept his mouth shut, then the fight never would have happened. But it did happen. There was nothing he could do to change that, and Trevor would have to come to terms with who he was.

Exhaustion crept up on him. Before long, he fought to stay awake, while the house slowly lit up from the emerging morning sun. Mark considered getting up and going out to look for Trevor, but before the idea could gain any serious ground, he was already asleep.

Mark woke up that afternoon to Trevor sitting on the end of the bed. He looked as fresh and bright as always.

"Morning," Trevor said.

"Welcome back." Mark yawned. "Where did you go?"

"Nowhere. Don't worry about it." Trevor dismissed the question. "I want to apologize. Maybe I blew things out of proportion."

"You think?" Mark sat up and stretched.

"Yeah, well, you didn't exactly take it well either," Trevor said, indicating the state Mark had left the house in after his fit. "I have to accept you for who you are. I understand that. I just get scared, I guess."

"Scared of what?"

"You're the only one I have left in the world, and I'm scared of losing you," Trevor said, and Mark realized the difficulty it took him to admit that. He appreciated it more than he could articulate at the moment.

"I'm not going anywhere without you." Mark put a hand on Trevor's leg.

"I'm glad. And besides, this whole bi-thing could just be a phase," Trevor said, putting his hand over Mark's.

Mark looked away. whatever small amount of comfort he felt at Trevor's apology falling away. "Yeah," he said, "maybe."

XXII.

The entire house smelled delicious. A fat turkey sat steaming on the dining room table, surrounded by a plethora of colors and textures: candied yams, cranberry sauce, a huge bowl of golden mashed potatoes, and thick brown gravy. All the places had been set; the holiday china gleamed in front of the seats. All but one. The Jensens sat quietly. LaVell expertly carved sheets of turkey while Clara fussed with baby Rachel. Caryn sat across from Isaac, both of whom had little to say. Once the plates had been filled, they bent their head in prayer.

At the end of the table sat an empty chair, devoid of even a setting. No plate, nor silverware. Even in spirit, Mark was not there. With minimal conversation, they ate their feast. In turn, they each avoided looking at the vacant chair.

After dinner, they moved into the living room. They sat around the television and had sporadic conversations. The sisters were visibly stiff with each other. Isaac served up the pie and whipped cream. He talked with his father about their plans to finish converting his room into Rachel's nursery, a project that had been put on hold when he had come back home.

Soon after, Caryn left and Isaac disappeared into his bedroom. LaVell continued to stare at the TV as his wife eventually cleaned the kitchen and put Rachel to bed. Alone, he sighed audibly. It had been the worst Thanksgiving he had ever experienced. The empty chair at the end of the table yawned at him like a vast hole. Inside of him as well. Today was supposed to be full of cooking and laughter, wearing thick sweaters while throwing a football around.

What if we were wrong? He wondered. *What if our attitudes were wrong and we handled Mark poorly? What if because of that, it's now too late?*

***

Hannah sat at the edge of the couch. Her feet tapped the carpet, the only vent to her restlessness. Her brothers sat on either side of her. They, along with all the other members of her family, were absorbed in the football game on TV. She hated football and couldn't be in less of a mood to deal with a room full of relatives, but she couldn't stand being alone in her room anymore. Because of the holiday, she felt obligated to spend time with family. Even if half didn't talk to her and the other half treated her like an oddity. Unable to sit through another round of verbal assaults flung at the referee, she left the room.

"Grab some turkey for me, would ya?" her brother Mitchell hollered at her. She ignored it. Instead she grabbed her coat

"Where are you going?" her mom asked.

"Out. I dunno, just going for a walk."

"It's Thanksgiving, dear."

"I know. I just want some air," she said. Her mom looked at her for a moment and then gave a small nod. Since she had been caught with Lindsey, things with her mom had gone from tense to politely cohabitating. Some days it was almost like before.

The street stretched quietly before her as she stepped out. It was the type of suburban quiet you only get on holidays. No traffic sounds, the still air, and only an occasional yell of children in a back yard. With no destination in mind, she turn up the first intersection she came too. Her mind in neutral, she wandered aimlessly.

After unaccounted minutes, she turned another corner and saw someone else walking her way. It annoyed her. She enjoyed the empty world she traveled through; it had calmness about it that she welcomed. As the person got closer, she recognized her.

"Hi," Jennifer said.

"Hi," Hannah replied. "Tired of family too?"

"Yeah. That and one of my younger cousins ate too much and threw up everywhere."

"Eww. I'd leave too." A moment of awkward silence filled the space between the two. "You're friends with Mark, right? Have you heard from him?" Lately, Hannah had wondered where Mark and Trevor had disappeared to more and more. There were days when she wished they had taken her with them.

"No. No one has. It's like Mark and Trevor fell off the face of the planet." They shared another silence, each with their own thoughts.

"Well, I should get back." Hannah started to walk off.

"We should hang out sometime," Jennifer said.

Hannah turned around said, "Listen, you're cute and all, but I…"

"Don't flatter yourself. I just want to hang out," Jennifer said with a small smile. Hannah's cheeks went red.

"Sorry. It's just been strange with people since I was outed. I would like to hang out sometime."

"Great! It's a date… well, you know," Jennifer said and continued her walk.

***

Aaron and Sandy Buell sat in front of the television. Sandy had packed away paper plates covered in tin foil into the refrigerator. Her aunt was always so generous with the leftovers. This year especially so, and she knew it was because of sympathy.

"It might be nice to take some of that food to the neighbors," Sandy said, letting her train of thought spill out of her mouth.

"They have their own food," her husband said without turning from the TV.

"I'm just saying that we'll never eat all that on our own. It's too much." She paused; he said nothing. "Trevor always took care of leftovers. He had quiet an appetite."

Aaron steadfastly continued to say nothing. His gaze remained locked onto the set in front of him. Sandy opened her mouth to say something but closed it again. Instead she sat on the couch until she couldn't hold it in any longer.

"It just didn't seem the same without Trevor this year. The day didn't feel complete. Don't you think?"

"Do you really think we need to take his sort around family?" Aaron said in a low voice.

"I suppose not," she said slowly. "I don't know. It just seemed off, not like a proper holiday. Didn't it seem different to you?"

He didn't reply, his silence growing weight. The muscles in his jaws moved. Knowing the signs, she went to bed without another word.

XXIII.

The days took on a new normal for Mark. Mostly he just sat in "his room" amongst the scattered tractor parts and boxes of old hot rod magazines, staring out the large multi-paned window. The light brown patina of the long, brittle grass in conjunction with the solid grey sky glowed too bright, reflected by clumps of icy snow that dotted the ground. He stared at it just the same. His mind ran on autopilot mostly. Time passed unnoticed. As he sat there, he brought himself from the pits of despair to the greatest of heights. His imagination conjured the drama of going home from acceptance to more rejection. Sometimes he and Trevor had made it to the big city. Sometimes they succeeded; other times they were in a back alley, used up and broken, hustling their own asses and burnt out.

If he wasn't contemplating the possibilities, his mind sat in neutral. When he wasn't doing that, he slept. Most of the time he slept wherever he happened to be, whether on the hard floor, their grubby mattress, or the dangerous couch. Trevor did quite a bit of sleeping as well; occasionally, he would stir and get high. Mark heard him leave a few times. Once, he came back with a bag of weed and McDonald's hamburgers. Mark didn't know how he had managed it and didn't care. The money that Sheila had given him went quickly. They had a few discussions about using the money to leave, but Trevor and his Tom Sawyer-like need for adventure quashed the idea. Mark just gave up. He haunted the house like a ghost. He would wake up at dawn, slip out of bed while Trevor slept, and wander about aimlessly before settling in his spot in front of the window. Trevor would wake up whenever he pleased then either leave or go back to sleep. Conversation between the two became short and sometimes tense. They argued more often than not.

When Trevor came back with food and weed again, Mark finally asked how he acquired it.

"I got hold of Luke. I'm dealing a little for him. The cut is complete crap, but it's better than nothing," Trevor said while attempting to roll a joint.

"We'd probably get more money if you didn't trade half of it for marijuana," Mark pointed out.

"Yeah, probably," Trevor said, unfazed. Mark rolled his eyes and went back into his room.

Mark had felt down before plenty of times. Depression wasn't completely new to him, but it went through quick dips before he found his way out of it. Reading helped the most, but he was out of books. This new sort of depression sunk its claws in deep and held him in place. His bones felt too heavy to move; not that he wanted to. The effort of movement, thought, or anything but breathing took too much to be worth it. Fueled by resignation to a hopeless fate and sustained by the idea of no escape, the black hole he sat in only deepened. Grasping at those ideas that used to make him happy only turned against him. They stoked a heatless fire inside, and it sunk him deeper in the emotional quagmire.

His only caveat, double-edged as it was, had slipped in as insidious as the depression. Apathy became his best friend. The gloom he sat with became bearable, almost welcome, with the lack of caring. It didn't matter that they were outcast. Nor did it matter that they would either starve or freeze to death before spring. Apathy warmed him and whispered laconically in his ear that it would be all right. It would be all right because what did it matter anyway? The pain of it went away when you didn't care.

***

This morning Trevor had gone again. He said something about lifting some food at the grocery store. Mark mumbled that this should be the last time. The clerk was starting to get suspicious. Time passed, as it is wont to do. As the shadows began to stretch, Trevor returned. He walked in and stood next to Mark for a moment, saying nothing. He dropped something on the floor and walked off. Mark looked over to see an astronomy magazine. A bright nebula, resplendent in reds and blues, gleamed on the cover. A rush of emotion came over him. He suddenly missed school and his former fantasies of the future. Most of all, he missed hope.

Apathy didn't make the caring go away; it simply numbed him from it. All that emotion still sat there. It just hid from him. Emotion sauntered back to him, and at the forefront came gratitude, followed by hope, and sauntering, slouched guilt.

"What's this for?" Mark asked standing and stretching.

"I know you're into that space stuff, so I grabbed it for you." Trevor emptied out his pockets.

227

More noodles, canned goods, and a few candy bars. "You were right. The clerks at the store are getting suspicious. We need to go somewhere different for food."

"There is nowhere different." Mark sighed.

"I know," Trevor said, his voice devoid of caring. Suddenly Mark had his arms around him a tight hug. When he was finally let go Trevor asked, "What was that for?"

"I think we take each other for granted sometimes," Mark said, holding his magazine like a revered object.

"It happens." Trevor shrugged it off.

He made dinner, for once. Mark went outside to get water for the noodles. The one-legged farmer stood at his own back door, watching him. Mark raised his hand in a polite wave. The distance made it hard to tell, but he was pretty sure the old coot just scowled at him. *Whatever*, Mark thought. *We've done pretty well for him. Mending fences and even cleaning up this shack. He has nothing to complain about.*

The boys ate by lantern light. Sitting carefully on the rickety couch, the sound of their chewing echoed around them.

"We're getting low on kerosene," Mark said between bites.

"We need to get out of here," Trevor said, tossing his plate down.

"I've been saying that since we moved in."

"I mean out of Cache and out of Idaho. Just get out. We talked about all these places we need to go, but they are still just as far away as always." Trevor stood.

"I wish you would have decided that when we had some extra money." It would have been easy for him to be bitchy about it, but Mark didn't want to ruin Trevor's sudden change of heart. If anything, he wanted to encourage it as much as possible. "Didn't we agree on Seattle?"

"Yeah, to start with. Things will be so different once we get there." Trevor had a faraway look on his face. After a thoughtful moment he said, "What if things change too much? What if we change, like completely?"

"We'd have to change a little bit, I suppose. That's the point. As long as you don't become some uber-fag," Mark joked.

"Would you still love me if I was a bitchy queen?" Trevor paraded in front of the lantern light, swishing to and fro.

"You are far too gay for that," Mark deadpanned. Trevor stopped in mid-swish and looked shocked.

"How can you say that?" he collapsed dramatically on the edge of the couch.

"Because you've been stuck up my ass since I met you."

"And here I thought you were a top," Trevor flailed a limp wrist at him. Mark stood up and rolled his eyes while taking his dish to the kitchen. "Seriously though. I think we come off as pretty straight, but once we get out of here, what if I do become a bitchy queen? Would you still stick around?"

Mark saw a more serious question behind Trevor's eyes, and he wasn't sure he could answer right now. As much as he loved his friend, he couldn't help but wonder how much of it truly was situational. They might not have been the only two queers in town, but they grew up protecting each other's secrets. And now they were outcasts together, planning an uncertain future that they were both reluctant to do anything about

"Someone has to keep your stupid ass out of trouble," Mark said and plopped down next to him. "As long as we're being serious, when are we getting out of here? It's getting colder, and we're getting broker. Pretty soon we're going to have to start eating the neighbor's dogs."

"We may have to. I'm tapped out."

"What about the stuff you're selling for Luke?" Mark hated to ask about it, but it was the only thing keeping them afloat at the moment.

"Um, yeah. I wouldn't count on that. I don't think he wants to bother trying to sell up here right now." Trevor said. Mark didn't buy it.

"That 'cut' you were getting, he wasn't selling you, was he? Skimming off the top for personal use?" Mark asked him.

"I honestly didn't think he would notice. That way we got the money, which wasn't much, and I got a little for my time and trouble." Trevor waved it off. "Anyway, I've got a better idea. Let's throw a party. We'll invite Fabiana and Anissa, a few other people, maybe even bring in some friends from Grason. We'll have a big ol' party, and after that party we leave."

"I'm for the party, but unless it's BYOB, it's going to be lame," Mark reasoned.

"We supply the place, and they supply the refreshments. After that we just pick up and leave."

"Still have no money. Don't forget that part," Mark said but smiled at Trevor's unending optimism.

"What if we rob our fat, worthless 'landlord'?" Trevor said. Mark waited for Trevor's trademark grin that always bookended the ridiculous ideas he came up with purely for entertainment purposes. It never showed.

"You cannot be serious." Mark was willing to do a lot of things, more so now than ever, but robbing someone outright drew a line he wasn't willing to cross. Not yet. "We'd be the first and last on the suspects list."

"We'd be long gone before he ever knew what hit him. The moment he left his house, we'd hit it and run. No one would be the wiser." Trevor was getting excited by his own idea.

"Our faces are up everywhere. Besides, I'm pretty sure that fat bastard owns guns. It's not worth it."

"You didn't have much of a problem coming with me to take Eli's camping equipment," Trevor pointed out. His tone dripped with disappointment that Mark didn't share his enthusiasm.

"That was different. That was for survival."

"Do you have any better fucking ideas?" Trevor stood up with a surprising explosion of anger. "There are no jobs to be had that last longer than an afternoon around here, and we are poor and hungry. This goddamn dirtpatch will kill us. It has been killing us since we were born. All I need to do is get enough money to get a bus out of here. We'll make enough for a couple of bus tickets and maybe a little extra. It's not like I want to take his entire life savings."

"Sure, whatever." Mark scoffed.

"Have a little goddamn faith in me!" Trevor screamed, his red eyes now streaming. "That's all I ever wanted. I just want to have someone to have a little faith in me. I'm not the screw-up everyone thinks I am."

"We sure as hell wouldn't be here if you weren't," Mark said and immediately regretted it.

"You didn't have to come along. In fact I wish you hadn't. There'd be a lot less bitching and complaining. I gave you your freedom. You would still be living a damned lie if it weren't for me."

"Trevor, I…"

"No, fuck you! You hate being here with me so much, you can fuck right off out the door!"

"Trevor, listen…"

"You listen. I'm not the degenerate here. I'm not the screw up. I'm not!"

By now Trevor's face was beet red and he was bawling openly. Mark walked up to him but Trevor shoved him away. Mark approached again, but this time Trevor let him. Mark wrapped him in his arms and held him as Trevor cried into his chest and shoulder.

"You aren't a fuck-up," Mark reassured him. "Neither one of us are. It's the world that's all screwed up. If it weren't, then we'd still be at home." Trevor blubbered something that Mark didn't catch.

XXIV.

Jennifer sat in a coffee shop, sipping on a steaming cup of hot chocolate. Across from her sat Hannah, nibbling on a brownie. The girls had both discarded their coats in the overly warm shop.

"Are you still on the lookout for Mark?" Hannah asked.

"Yeah. I did some asking around, checked with the Salvation Army even. No one has seen him." Jennifer swished her cocoa around.

Mark and Trevor had been gone long enough that most of their classmates had already moved on from it. Besides a few acquaintances that had been close to the boys, including Jennifer, Hannah and some of the soccer team, most people didn't pay their disappearance much mind after the first couple of weeks. Now that time had stretched to months.

"Pretty sure he doesn't want to be found," Hannah said. "I don't blame him. I thought about running away too, when I got caught with Lindsey."

"Why didn't you?"

"I didn't have the guts, I guess. I envy those two a little bit. Mark's a smart guy, though. I'm sure he's doing okay," she said in an effort to be reassuring. She knew how Jennifer felt about Mark, even though they had never spoken of it.

"I know. But if he's with Trevor, God only knows. I feel bad for saying it, but Trevor has a tendency to leap before he looks."

"He's not so bad, just a little impulsive. Don't worry about it." Hannah split her brownie in half and slid one part of it to Jennifer. "So how long have you been holding on to this crush for Mark?"

Jennifer started to protest then sighed. "Since, like, junior high. It's stupid. I've known he was gay for a long time, but I still can't help it. You probably think I'm an idiot."

"Yes," Hannah smiled, "but I'm sure you're not the first straight girl to fall for a donut-puncher. You ever tell him how you feel?"

"No. Not really. Plus, what's the use? It's not like he feels the same." Jennifer took a big bite of the proffered brownie.

"You'd be surprised."

"What's that supposed to mean?"

"The rules of attraction are more fluid than you think. Maybe you'd be that one girl in the entire world he would be attracted to." Hannah brushed hair out of her face. Jennifer just scoffed.

"I seriously doubt that."

"Do you doubt the words of a fellow queer? I firmly believe that people are attracted to people, to a person. Gender is relative." Hannah stood up. "I'm going to be a bad Mormon and order a coffee. What's the worst that can happen?"

Jennifer rolled her eyes and shook her head. As Hannah stood at the counter, waiting to give her order, Jennifer sat there and thought about what she'd said. She wasn't sure she completely understood it. It was one or the other, male or female, right?

"You think he's bi?" Jennifer asked once Hannah came back with a steaming cup of sweet black coffee.

Hannah shrugged as she took a careful sip. "No idea. All I'm saying is people put too much into the idea that it only goes one way. Just because you are straight, doesn't mean that at some point you wouldn't find another woman attractive. It doesn't make you suddenly gay, or even bi. You just happen to be attracted to that particular girl."

"If I were anybody else, I'd say you were hitting on me with talk like that." Jennifer laughed.

"I've learned my lesson. I'm not hitting on anyone until I get as far away from Grason as possible. And besides, you were one of the few straight girls that weren't afraid to talk to me or tried to flirt with me after I got caught."

"Flirt with you? Like who?" Jennifer never was one for gossip but she couldn't resist.

"Oh my God! It was ridiculous. Half the girls who shunned me after I was outed would secretly text me or get me alone and chat me up. Might as well have been open season on me."

"There are that many lesbians at school?"

"Not really. Just straight girls who want to see what it's like to kiss a girl.'"

"Like Lindsey?" Jennifer asked then regretted it.

"No, definitely not like Lindsey. Lindsey has to figure that out on her own," Hannah said, staring into her coffee.

The girls lapsed into silence, each sipping at their beverages. The jingle of the bell above the door made Jennifer look up with mild interest.

"Hey, isn't that Mark's brother Isaac?" she whispered.

"I think so. I wonder how he's been dealing with all this." Hannah wondered out loud.

***

Isaac had gone into the coffee shop because he had skipped breakfast and wanted to grab a quick muffin. His day started with the sound of food being prepared in the kitchen. Despite the promise of breakfast, something seemed off. The house felt cool and haunted. He stretched but refused to get out of bed until he figured out what was wrong. Minutes ticked by, and still he couldn't put his finger on it. Giving up, he emerged from his blankets and put his slippers on. As soon as he opened the bedroom door and smelled the pancakes, it hit him. Today was Mark's birthday. Today, his little brother turned sixteen. Grimly, his mother went about making Mark's favorite breakfast of pancakes and bacon. He found his father staring at a newspaper, the same dark countenance about him.

Isaac sat at the table, drinking a glass of orange juice and waiting for his plate of steaming food. No one spoke. No one acknowledged anything more than what which lay in front of them. It was maddening.

"Mark turns sixteen today," he finally said. All he got from his parents were affirming grunts and nods of heads. "You think if he smells this delicious breakfast, he'll come back?" To that he only received more silence. "Do you even want him to come back?"

Clara dropped a plate full of food. The plate shattered, and pancakes and bacon scattered. She stomped off and locked herself in her room. LaVell continued to wordlessly stare at his paper. Isaac stood up and cleaned up the mess. Once finished, he dressed and left the house.

Maybe it's time to go back to school. Or maybe it's time I finally find my brother. "I wonder how he's spending his birthday," he wondered aloud as he walked into the coffee shop.

XXV.

Mark dropped a baggy on Trevor's lap as he lounged in bed. He knew that Trevor had a secret stash and where it had been the whole time, he'd just played dumb up until now. "Spark it up."

"Hey, I was going to tell you we had some left." Trevor smiled while he started sorting out seeds and stems.

"Uh huh. Whatever. I just don't feel like being sober today," Mark said, sitting next to him.

"You've been awfully mopey today. What gives?"

"It's my birthday."

"Oh shit! I'm so sorry. I forgot." Trevor immediately began apologizing. "Here, the day isn't over yet. We're still going to make this the best day yet. We're doing that party tonight. I can get the girls and have them rally up some people. Entrance fee is whatever can mess us up."

Ryan had been nice enough to leave them some rolling papers. Mark took them from Trevor. Regardless of how much more experience Trevor had, Mark found out that he could roll a much better joint

241

than his friend. They sat and smoked while the cogs in Trevor's head turned and turned. At this point Mark would normally warn him not to get stupid, but he was beyond caring. He could settle for stupid. He was supposed to be in school, supposed to be in seminary, supposed to be wondering if his parents would be able to send him on a mission in a few years. Instead he sat on a ratty mattress in an abandoned house, smoking weed.

"Screw it," he mumbled as he passed the joint back. *No NASA for me,* he conceded. *Just an outcast living on the fringes. I don't fit in at home. I seriously doubt I would fit in there. Hell, I don't fit in here.*

"Yeah, screw it," Trevor belatedly agreed as smoke roiled from his mouth.

"Do you ever feel like your entire life has just been nothing more than keeping secrets?" Mark asked.

"Of course. Those secrets are what got us in this trouble," Trevor pointed out.

"Yeah, but sometimes I think that after a while, keeping secrets just becomes second nature to us. Like we can't stop doing it."

"Why? What else are you keeping from me?" Trevor asked in seriousness.

Mark looked at him and contemplated reopening the previous debacle of his bisexuality. He didn't want another blowout with Trevor. He knew that the shaggy boy had his own reality that didn't exactly coincide with the actual one. It made it easier for him to believe only the things he wanted. It hurt Mark to think that Trevor, the only person he had, might not be the right one to talk about it with.

"Say something. What is it?" Trevor said, breaking him from his thoughts. There was a genuine look of concern. Mark wasn't sure how to start. "Let me guess, you've been a closet Catholic this whole time?" Trevor covered his concern with play. "You're straight, you're hiding food in your butt, you're secretly a millionaire."

Mark shook his head at them all.

"You want to be trapped in the middle of nowhere with someone else?" Mark could hear a real fear in that sentence. Not that he wasn't sure what tomorrow would bring but that he would have no one there when it came.

"It's nothing. Honest," Mark blew it off. "Let's plan a party. Make sure someone brings some food. Neither of us have eaten in a couple days."

Hiding his relief poorly, Trevor quickly dressed and disappeared. In his absence, Mark started picking up and cleaning the best he could. It didn't matter how much work he put in it, the house still looked like crap. It kept him busy, and at least he could say he did his best. As he worked, he became excited to have people over.

Hours later, Mark heard a car pull up outside. He put aside the astronomy magazine, something he had read cover to cover many times over by now. Trevor bounded through the door, holding a twelve pack of Natural Light beer. Behind him walked in Fabiana and Anissa. Anissa still dressed as Ernesto, but she had a bag over her shoulder containing her freedom as Anissa.

"Happy birthday," Anissa called out. She handed him a covered dish. "My mom had some leftover enchiladas. Nothing beats a birthday enchilada."

"Happy birthday," Fabiana said and kissed him on the cheek as she passed. Mark felt his face redden. "Better eat that quickly. Trevor has been trying to get at it."

"Ryan is coming over later, and he said that he'll have a couple friends with him, so this should be fun." Trevor beamed.

For the first time in a couple months, Mark felt warm inside. He leaned against the counter and began eating the heavenly food out of the dish. He shared some with Trevor, who tried to convince Fabiana to let her mother adopt him, if only for her cooking.

Anissa emerged from the bathroom wearing tight, tapered-leg jeans and a very becoming sweater. "I was going to wear a skirt, but it gets too damn cold in here."

"Looks good to me, sis," Fabiana told her. "Hey, stick the beer outside so it stays cold," she commanded Trevor. Dutifully he complied. Anissa walked by and he stopped her.

"You okay? Something is off with you." Trevor pulled a face of mock scrutiny.

"I'm fine," she brushed him off playfully but even Mark could see that something was up.

"It's that asshole, Daniel. He was giving her a bunch of crap again. Threatening to 'beat his faggot ass,' I believe his exact words were," Fabiana said.

245

From the look on her face, Mark felt fairly sure she was ready to bury the guy in a deep hole.

"What if he knows?" Anissa asked her sister. "To him, I'm just a queer boy. If he found out about this," she ran her hand around her body, "he'd probably do worse that just push me around."

"Don't worry about it," Trevor said, putting his arm across her shoulders. "He's probably just a closet case. If he saw all this, he'd want to hit it. But not with his fists." Trevor thrust his pelvis a couple times for emphasis.

"Crude," Anissa pushed him away in pretend offense while the rest giggled.

***

By the time Ryan had pulled up to their house, Mark already had a decent buzz. Anissa had produced an iPod and battery-powered speakers, and they all took turns dancing. He wasn't much of a dancer, but they managed to pull the birthday boy up and he joined them as they swung and moved. The girls mock-flirted with him as he showed off his overly-white dance skills.

Ryan walked in holding a quarter-empty bottle of vodka. "Let's get this party started," he announced. "I'm sure my mom won't miss one bottle." He took a large swig from it then handed it to Trevor, who wasted no time going to stand next to him. "I brought some guests." Behind him came a well-built teen in a lettered jacket.

"Lance, I told you, I can't stay long. My parents think I'm at a church function," said a girl next to him. The voice sounded familiar to Mark, but he couldn't immediately place it. It wasn't until Ryan moved out of the way that he saw her.

"Lindsey?" She looked up, and there was a sudden panic in her eyes.

"Holy shit," Trevor said, reeling back. "One of Grason's many pariahs. We should start a club." He swept his arm around majestically.

"Hi, Trevor. Is this where you're living?" She tried deftly to deflect the attention.

"Welcome to our castle," he enunciated in a horrible British accent.

"And by 'castle,' he means hovel." Mark grinned. Lindsay stood next her boyfriend trying to avoid eye contact with either of the boys.

"It's not bad for a hovel," said another voice just behind the couple. "Could use a little paint, new carpets, maybe a fire."

"Jennifer! Look, all of Grason is coming to see you," Trevor called out to Mark.

She rushed past Trevor to Mark. "Everyone has been wondering where you went." She gave him a big hug.

She smelled wonderful, and he became uncomfortably aware that the only way he had been able to wash himself or his clothes in the last couple months was an old bucket they'd found, cold water, and a giant bar of soap they'd lifted from the store. She held him tight despite the fact that he tried to break away, fearing that he smelled bad.

"How did you know I was here?" Mark asked her.

"Ryan's my cousin. He told me about a party with some new friends he made. Sounded like fun to me." Her eyes sparkled as she talked.

"I swear to God, all LDS family trees are nothing but a telephone pole," Mark joked.

"Everyone has been worried about you." She finally released him. Now he wished she hadn't let go.

"I doubt that," Trevor sneered.

"Both of your parents were looking for you, pretty much everywhere." Trevor didn't say anything but Mark knew what he was thinking. Trevor didn't believe his parents went looking for him, or if they did, they didn't try very hard. "Your brother even left school early." She turned back to Mark.

"What? Isaac?" An immense wave of guilt crested above him, threatening to crash down. Maybe he'd judged his brother unfairly. His parents wouldn't want him to quit BYU just to look for their queer kid. Maybe Isaac wasn't the "golden boy" he had built him up to be.

"Yeah, soon as he heard, he got a ride back up to Grason. He was really adamant about trying to find you." Mark watched her as she talked. The sense of relief of finding him was plain.

"Well, if they want us back so bad, they shouldn't have given us the boot in the first place," Trevor announced, the bottle of vodka in his hand. "We are masters of our own destiny here. We're moving on anyway. Big city, here we come."

"Which one?" Fabiana asked.

"All of them," he said then took a heroic swig off the bottle.

**

The evening wore on into deep night, and the teenagers continued to party. Fabiana taught all the white kids colorful swears in Spanish while Anissa went between smoking weed and trying to catch the vodka bottle before it was all gone. Mark continued to drink the cheap beer and take a perverse delight in how uncomfortable Lindsey looked around them. Her boyfriend asked what Trevor's previous comment about her being pariah was about, but she refused to answer him.

Trevor became unusually clingy with Mark after everyone had arrived. He made a point of sitting near him, had his arm around his shoulders, and plainly refused to let him out of sight. As the inebriation settled in, he would steal an occasional kiss from Mark. Everyone assumed that the two of them were together, and in a way he assumed the same thing. Somewhere between buzzed and drunk, Trevor's attention began to settle on Ryan. Mark didn't mind. By that point he was beginning to feel a little smothered.

Everyone had gathered in the large bedroom they shared. The girls had landed on one corner of the bed, talking and giggling amongst themselves. The boys were standing around at the other corner. Mark sat on the hard floor, his back against the wall, watching and sipping on his beer. Between the intoxication and the being around people, Mark felt good. He didn't feel the need to talk or laugh, just to be.

Jennifer caught Lindsey up on school gossip. Lindsey looked relieved to not have Lance pawing at her. Mark kept looking over at Jennifer in spite himself. The boys suddenly got a little quieter as Lance pulled a small ball of tin foil out of his pocket. With it he pulled a tiny glass pipe. He opened the metal ball, and Mark could just make out a little bit of white inside it. *Why is it jocks always have meth when they can afford something much better?* Mark thought bitterly.

As the other boys disappeared into the bathroom, Mark carefully stood up and went outside. The night wasn't as cold as most, or at least he couldn't feel it as much as he sat on the cracked step. Whether because of the alcohol and drugs, he couldn't be sure, but he felt so conflicted. He looked up at the crystal clear sky. There were so many stars that it looked impossible. Raw wonder mixed with the alcohol, and his mind boggled at the sight. He fought for concentration to locate constellations.

The door opened behind him, and Anissa sat next to him on the step. "Any sign of the mothership?"

"Nope. Just a few random ones looking for yokels to probe," he said. Anissa laughed, and then they fell silent. "It is gorgeous up there." He pointed at the sky.

"It scares me. Space. The thought of all that nothing being up there frightens me." Anissa admitted.

"There is a lot of nothing up there, but look at that sky. There is a lot of somethings, and it's fascinating. Look at that one, for instance." He pointed at a particularly bright twinkling star nearly straight up. "That one is called Vega. It's twice as massive as our sun, meaning it would fill up a good portion of our sky during the day if we were orbiting it. 'Course, we'd be dead because of the heat and radiation."

"That's pleasant."

"But it's also younger than our sun. It burns white, not yellow, and will most likely die out before our sun does. It was one of the first stars we started gathering information on." Mark sat there, and Anissa looked over at him. He had a look of peace..

"Do you think it has any planets?" she asked.

"Probably not. It has a disk of dust and gas around it that are probably proto- planets that smashed together. Whatever planets it might have had would have gotten bombarded."

"And here I thought all the fun was inside. You're having your own out here. You know that this is your party, right?"

"And I'll cry if I want to," Mark said. "You know, I don't even know what that means."

"I think it's a song or something. So what's up? You got all moody." She nudged him again. Mark appreciated the concern.

"It's nothing. Just have a lot on my mind. Maybe a bit overwhelmed. I mean, we've been on our own, and to suddenly have all these people around is almost too much."

"Especially people from your old life?"

"Yeah. I never did get too close to Lindsey, but Jennifer and I have known each other for a long time." He reached out to the stars, as if touching the sky would make it ripple like water.

"I've seen the way you look at Jennifer. You like her." She gave him a nudge. "I don't blame you. She is nice. And pretty."

"Do you like her?" Mark asked. "I mean, being transgender, I assumed you liked guys, but I never thought to ask. Sorry."

She laughed at his sudden embarrassment. "I like who I like. I mean, yeah, I'm all about the boys, but if I came across the right girl, then maybe. Who knows? If you weren't with Trevor, I'd show you how much I like boys."

"Am I Trevor's, though? I'm never really sure if we're with each other or stuck with each other. It's hard to tell with him."

"But what about your feelings for Jennifer?"

"I'm not supposed to like girls; it's not the way gay works," he said sarcastically.

"Attraction isn't something you can control. It is what it is." She took thoughtful sip from her can of beer.

"That's not really reassuring."

Anissa shrugged. "Be attracted to who you want, and don't worry about how it's supposed to fit. People get too hung up labels and putting people in a box. Maybe you're bi, or maybe you just happen to be attracted to this one person who is a girl."

"I don't think Trevor would be as understanding."

"I know you two have history and everything, but you have to look out for yourself. He is. He may care for you, but at the end of the day, he's looking out for Trevor."

"He's not that way," Mark weakly defended.

"Oh? Right now he's tweeking with Lance and Ryan in your bathroom. I can guarantee you that while Lance is puffing away, Trevor is sucking face with Ryan. And as straight as Lance is, he's too high to care."

Mark sighed and flung his empty beer can into the dark. Looking back up to the infinite night, he said, "Yeah, I do like Jennifer, and I probably have for a while. It's tough to think you are one thing for so long only to realize you are really something else. It doesn't make much sense."

"Who said anything about it having to make sense? Just go with it," Anissa said with a big smile as she stood and went back into the house.

Mark sat there with his swirling thoughts. *Should I be jealous of Trevor and Ryan?* he wondered. *Should I be upset he's doing a drug that I would have ended our friendship over back in Grason? Should I just go in and start flirting with Jennifer?* He decided that another beer was much better than thinking about any of it and went in search of one.

"You want some?" Ryan offered the glass pipe full of skeletal smoke as Mark walked back inside. Mark shook his head and sat on the bed next to Jennifer. She gave him a concerned look, but he shook his head and smiled to reassure her. He watched Trevor crowded in the bathroom with the others. The tiny glass pipe went back and forth between Ryan, Trevor, and Lance.

"We should play spin the bottle," Ryan said, emerging from the bathroom and laying down the empty vodka bottle.

"Screw that, let's just play dare." Fabiana laughed.

"Screw that, let's screw," Trevor called out and then fell upon Ryan. Without hesitation the two of them became a mass of hands and lips.

Mark felt his chest tighten and a sharp knife cut through his buzz. His breathing became shallow as he became unsure what to do. Should he stand and leave, or join, or make a scene? Should he just sit and watch? Should he grab someone and do the same? As everyone yelled and catcalled, his fog cleared by a soft hand on his.

"Let's go sit in the other room." Jennifer stood up and led him away.

They went to his room and sat looking out the window. The raucous sounds from the other room penetrated the walls, and he tried to blot it out. He felt the room start to spin, so he closed his eyes, but it only got worse.

"You want this?" he handed her the can. She took a drink and put it on the floor.

"He's an ass," she said after a moment.

"He is, but we've gone this far."

"How could he just make out with some dude in front of you?"

"We're not really together. We're just in this together," he said more for his own benefit than hers.

"Still, I can tell it hurts." She put a calming hand his chest.

He sighed deeply and lay down. He felt horrible. His spinning head started to affect the sloshing contents of his stomach. He felt a ground-in dinginess that he couldn't take anymore.

"It's just too much, you know? I feel so far away from everything, like this is Limbo. No love, no warmth, no comfort or joy."

"There's always hope, right?" she asked, laying her head next to his.

"Look around; there's no room for hope here."

"That's not right," she whispered. He turned his head, and their eyes locked. "It's such a shame you're gay."

He said nothing, but their gaze never wavered. Slowly she got closer until their lips touched. Mark let it happen. His feelings for her were complicated, but right now he needed anything that could make him feel whole again. He hadn't felt whole since before they left Grason, and her soft, warm lips were a welcome respite from the cold winter that had been settling both in and around him. She felt alien and comfortable at the same time, and he finally gave himself to it. Her hand tentatively started to move across his ribs when the door suddenly burst open, the light from the other room momentarily blinding him.

"Ooooh!" Fabiana howled. "Trevor! It looks like she's taking him over to the dark side."

Trevor's head popped up over her shoulder. His lopsided grin was red from Ryan's stubble. "Save some for me. I'm going to need some of that later," he called out loudly.

Mark lay there frozen, stunned at being caught. It took a moment to realize that Trevor had disappeared as quickly as he appeared, apparently unfazed and uncaring. Fabiana winked at them then shut the door.

"I'm sorry," Jennifer said looking at him again, in the dark.

"Don't be." This time he reached for her.

XXVI.

The sun blinded him when he woke up, while his head pounded and his stomach roiled. He heard a sound to his left, and he looked over despite the pain. Jennifer stood by the door, pulling her long auburn hair into a ponytail. Images of last night paraded through his head.

"You look like hell," she said quietly.

"I feel like it," he croaked.

"I'm sorry, but I have to go. I'm probably going to be in trouble as it is." Mark nodded and then regretted it. She put her hand on the knob then stopped. "About last night...I mean, you were pretty into it for a gay guy."

"I'm not gay." he said thickly.

"Wait. Did I just turn you straight?"

"No," he managed a weak smile. After a moment of careful thought he continued, "I still like guys, a lot. But I like girls too."

"So are you a gay guy who likes chicks?"

"Not really."

"So I turned you bi," she said playfully.

"I was already there. It just took me running away to the wilderness to find out." He tried to smile at his joke, but it immediately turned into a wince. "Ugh, I hurt too much to think about it right now, but I know I had a good time."

"I did too." She smiled back and then grew serious. "Why don't you come back to Grason? You don't belong here. I'm sure if you went back you could work it out with your parents."

"This is purgatory. I was led here because this is where I belong," he said then leaned over and violently retched.

Quickly, Jennifer left the room. Once he stopped, she came back in to check on him then said goodbye. He rolled over and lay there until he couldn't stand the smell of his own vomit anymore. He crawled out of the room. Trevor lay snoring in bed. Judging by the state of it, he hadn't spent the night in it alone. Outside, he heard a car drive off. He assumed it to be Ryan. Feeling like dried up death, Mark found something to cover his vomit with and went back to sleep in the living room.

***

When Trevor woke up with the long shadows, he felt wrung out. He was surprised he been able to fall asleep last night, yet somehow he managed to get a few hours. He called out for Mark but got no answer. He crawled out of bed and stepped outside to urinate. Mark sat on the front step smoking a cigarette.

"That one of mine?" Trevor asked.

"I don't know. Someone left them." He handed the pack to Trevor who immediately took one out and lit it.

"Some crazy party, right?" Trevor said. Mark just grunted. They both watched their respective exhales float on the wind. "What was all that with you and Jennifer last night?"

"What was that with you and Ryan?" Mark accused. "You two seemed to be all sorts of friendly last night. Did you sleep with him?"

"We might have fooled around a little. I'm sorry, but I was pretty messed up last night. And besides, you ran off with Jennifer and played kissy face with her. What did you expect me to do?"

"I don't know. I don't know anything right now. I'm never sure if we're a couple or just friends. But I guess you made that clear when you jumped onto Ryan." Mark wanted to sound as angry and betrayed as he felt, but didn't have the energy. Instead it came out in an apathetic drone.

"You know me and who I am. I don't know what we are. I never really thought of it. You are mine, I know that, whatever form it takes. How do you think I felt when I saw you making out with Jennifer?"

"You didn't seem that affected by it at the time."

"I was high and horny. I can't be held accountable for my actions." He attempted a joke, but Mark didn't laugh. "Oh, that's right, I forgot you're bisexual now." His voice dripped with derision.

"Oh, so we're going to have this fight again." Mark sighed. "You make this entire process so much harder."

"Process? Either you know or you don't. It's easy."

"No, dammit. Listen Trevor. For once, just listen. It isn't easy, and the problem is, the only one I have to talk about it with is you."

"What's that supposed to mean? I've always been there for you."

"Yes, you have, but it's so hard to talk to you sometimes."

"You really think I'm that hard to talk to? You couldn't come to me?" The hurt in Trevor's voice was real. Mark had never heard it before.

"I'm sorry. It's just difficult."

"I understand. I really do. But you can talk to me about it. We've been under a lot of pressure, and I'm not the easiest person." Trevor put his arm around Mark as he apologized. "I'm sorry. I really am. You are the only person I've got, and I know I should treat you better. I just wish you didn't have to go and bang a chick to be sure."

"That wasn't what happened. I wanted validation by talking it out with someone. But you aren't the most receptive. I didn't 'bang' Jennifer for the validation. I'm attracted to her, and sometimes with you I feel so goddamn alone." Mark's words stung like a slap to the face.

"I'm sorry." Trevor sighed after an awkward moment of silence. "I really am sorry. It is a lot to take. Since we were little kids, it's always been the two of us. There aren't too many people who seem to fit me like you do. With all that's gone on, I guess I thought if you weren't like me, then you wouldn't want to be around me anymore. We have nothing, and I felt like all we've worked for was for nothing. Kicked out of our houses and exiled from our families. All we have is each other. I don't want to lose that."

"We do have each other, but just because I'm not strictly gay doesn't mean that I'm any different. I'm still just as attracted to guys as I ever was. I mean, I didn't have all those soccer players up on the wall of my room just because I like to play soccer. But it turns out that I'm attracted to girls too. It's who I am, and it would mean so much to me if you could be accepting of that."

"Honestly, I don't know. It might take me a while to get used to. I'm still not sure about the whole girls thing, but I love you no matter what you are. Just give me some time." The sincerity in Trevor's voice touched Mark. He grabbed Trevor's hand and held it.

"So, Jennifer, huh? How long you have you been waiting to tap that?" Trevor brought back his usual playful manner. Mark rolled his eyes, but couldn't stop a grin from emerging. Trevor was trying and he was grateful for it.

"I've been attracted to her for a while," he answered.

"Oh yeah? Who else?"

"Jeordie Ward's older sister."

"I could see that. You do have a thing for the dangerous type," Trevor said smugly while pulling on the collar of his leather jacket.

XXVII.

Days had passed since their party. The boys
were snoozing on the mattress when they heard a sound
outside. Sadness followed Fabiana as she walked in the
house. Her eyes were red and her head down. Ryan
followed her in, quiet for once. Without a word from
either one they shuffled past the boys and settled
carefully on the edge of the couch. Mark swallowed
down jagged pieces of jealousy at the sight of Ryan.

"You guys look like someone shat in your
shoe," Mark said. Fabiana sighed.

"It's been a bad couple of days," Ryan said
before lapsing back into silence. He waited for Fabiana
to say something first.

"Ernesto…Anissa got sent away." The boys
stood in shocked silence. "It started when that puta
madre Daniel came up to her after school. Somehow he
found out that Anissa was transgender. I don't know
how. By the time I made it outside, there was a circle
on the lawn of people watching. Daniel had her down
on the ground, slapping and hitting her. His pendejo
friends were throwing panties at her and laughing."

"Jesus. Poor Anissa," Mark said quietly. "Is she okay?"

"More or less. When we got home, my parents had a fit. Mama cried over her poor boy, and our father was pissed that his boy didn't try to fight back. Apparently the fact that I punched two of those dicks was an insult to his fatherly pride. That's when the argument started.

"Finally it was too much, and Anissa screamed at him. She told him, 'I'm not your boy. I'm your daughter. You've had two daughters all along and didn't even know it.' After that it got real quiet, and I wasn't sure what was going to happen."

"I could hear it all the way from my house," Ryan said, staring at his fingernails.

"Mama and I were sent to tend to the bruises. He disappeared for a while. I could hear him on the phone, but not what he said," Fabiana continued.

"Did he call the cops?" Trevor asked.

"No. Daniel's father is a cop. It wouldn't do any good," Ryan said. None of them could argue against it.

Fabiana took a deep breath. "I've never questioned it, never once. Ever since she came out as transgender, I considered her my sister. But in that moment, I wished she were just gay. It may not have gone any better, but maybe it would have. Maybe there would have been less hate."

"What did your parents do? Where did Anissa go?" Mark asked. Now that the shock was wearing off, he began to miss her already. He had few friends, and the subtraction of even one left a hole.

"Austin. There is an uncle there," Ryan said.

"Yeah. Uncle George will take in Ernesto." Fabiana wiped a tear away.

"But will he take in Anissa as well?" Mark asked.

"He is more open-minded, but he probably won't understand it at first. It's a safer place, and that's what matters. He's family."

A profound silence enveloped them. Mark thought of his family. He wondered if his sister had been born yet and if Isaac had thought to come this far out to look for him. He missed them and felt angry with them at the same time. A large part of him wanted to go home, but the anger kept him away. He was thankful that it never got violent at his house, but in a way he wished it did. Maybe it would help to burn off the resentment.

"I wish we'd had a chance to say goodbye first," Trevor said breaking the silence. They all mumbled agreement before Fabiana stood up.

"I need to get home. I just thought you guys should know." Ryan stood up with her and they left.

"Poor Anissa," Mark said plopping down on the couch where Fabiana had been sitting. He immediately shifted as a spring poked him in the butt. "I hate it here."

"Me too. I hate being hungry. When did we last eat?"

"Yesterday, I think." As if to confirm it, Mark's stomach began to grumble. Outside, the wind began to pick up. It quickly penetrated the walls, dropping the temperature inside the house. He stood and walked over the can of kerosene. "Better get the heater going. It's going to be a cold one."

"You sure you don't want to wait until dark?"

"Doesn't matter. We're out." Mark held the can up and shook it for effect. "Fuck!" he yelled in a sudden fit of anger. He drop kicked it, and it bounced off the wall with a loud echo. Mark continued to scream and stomp about the place. Trevor said nothing and just watched him, letting his friend get it all out. There was nothing he could say to make it better. Mark eventually ran out of steam and the two of them once again sat on the couch. They sat in silence as the day passed and continued to get colder.

"We might as well get in bed. We'll me more comfortable in the sleeping bags. Besides I just want to sleep." Trevor said.

"Me too. Maybe forever," Mark agreed and followed him.

***

The next morning the boys woke early. Early winter weather, as unpredictable as ever, rallied and stormed all night. But as the morning sun came up, the air turned calm and the snow settled into small drifts in the night. They were standing in living room when the kitchen door suddenly wrenched open and the overstuffed farmer hobbled in, his crutch leaving indents in the floor.

"At least you haven't burnt the place down." He scrutinized the place and then turned his attention to them. "You gotta go. I want you out of here."

"Why?" Mark asked, his face flush.

"Doesn't matter why. It's my place, and I say it's time to leave." The farmer clomped his way past them and peeked into the bed rooms.

"We have nowhere to go. It's winter out there." Mark followed him. Trevor sprang forward and put a hand on Mark's arm but it was shrugged off. "We cleaned the place up. We fixed your fences and paid you money. Everything you wanted, we did."

"I haven't gotten a dime from you in weeks. Plus I know you had parties, didn't ya? I told you not to do that, and you did." He swatted an empty beer can with the end of this crutch.

"One party. We had one, and nothing was damaged." Spittle flew from Marks lips. Trevor tried to calm him down, but it fell on deaf ears. "This is bullshit. We've made this death trap better in the few months we've lived here."

The farmer turned and faced the teen. His breath sour in Mark's face. "I don't need two damn runaways dying of exposure on my property. I don't

272

care where you queers go, just get your shit and leave. Now." He held Mark's gaze. Neither backed down.

"You got something against queers?" Mark growled.

"I couldn't care less. I just hate freeloading no-good shits like you."

"Hey," Trevor said getting between them. "Can we work something out? I'm sure you have some other things you want done around here."

"Screw him and screw this place. I'd rather lived in a ditch than anywhere near this piece of shit." Every word from Mark's mouth dripped with venom. Trevor had never once seen his friend in a fight, let alone try and start one. The farmer's face remained unreadable under his bushy, unkempt beard.

With speed neither knew he possessed, he swung a bloated hand and caught Mark on the side of his head. Mark stumbled from the blow. Trevor rushed the old man but ran into the upraised end of the crutch. He fell back as it knocked all the air from him. Mark stood up only to take the same crutch in the face.

"Get the hell out. If you're still here when I come back, I'm calling the police. Then you little assholes will be their problem." He clomped away.

Trevor had just got his breath back when he lunged forward. Mark caught him and pulled him back. "Screw it. Let's get out of here. We've stayed here too long anyway."

He let Trevor go and began stuffing balled up clothes in his backpack. Trevor reluctantly did the same. In five minutes they had everything packed. Mark made sure to pack the magazine Trevor had given him. The only extra thing Trevor had to pack was an earring that Anissa had left the night of the party. He wondered if they could go to Austin too. Maybe hitchhike there.

Mark went to the kitchen. On the counter sat the cooking equipment they had taken from Eli's garage.

"What about this stuff?" he asked. He turned to see Trevor standing in the middle of the living room, pissing on the floor. "What are you? Four years old?"

"Who cares? It's the least I could do for that fat turd." Mark couldn't argue with that sort of logic right now. "And leave that stuff. I was never going to give it back to Eli anyway."

Both boys shouldered their bags and walked out the door. They walked down the lane, side by side.

Once the old man's house came into view they lifted their middle fingers to it. They walked past, finger up the whole time. They reached the road, and on instinct, started walking towards the small gas station at the end of the mile. Trevor looked up at his friend.

"Does it hurt?" He gingerly touched an angry bruise blossoming on his friend's cheek.

Mark flinched. "Only when you do that."

"Now what?" Trevor asked.

"Isn't that my line? I thought you were always the one with the good ideas."

"We could hitchhike somewhere. We could be in Seattle in a couple of days. Austin in a week. Check up on Anissa then head to New York or something." Trevor had that old surety in his voice again.

"And how do we do that? Give out hand jobs? That is, provided some long-haul psycho doesn't chop us up and wear our skin as a dress. I'm not like you."

"What the hell is that supposed to mean?"

"Nothing. Forget it." Mark continued to trudge along but Trevor stopped.

"If you have something to say, then say it."

Mark stopped and turned, "I know what you and Luke were up to on the ride to Cache. It was a cheap shot, and I'm sorry I said it. C'mon, let's go."

"Where?" Trevor yelled. "Home?"

"Yes," he answered before he realized what he was going to say. "Yes, go back home. We're tired, hungry, and cold. I'm sick of this life, and most of the time I just want to curl up and die. At this point I don't care if they accept me or not. That's their problem, not mine. All I want is an actual meal, a hot shower, and a real bed. If they don't let me in the door, then I'm going to my aunt's house."

"Oh, that's fine for you, now that you are all bisexual and shit. You can just go home and date Jennifer, and your parents will be happy as pigs in slop. You can hide behind that. What about me? There is no way my dad is ever going to let me anywhere near the house again. As far as he's concerned, I'm dead." Trevor flung his arms wide as he yelled, and his jacket jingled.

"You and I have been living like savages for months. Don't you think if I was going to hide behind anything, I would have done it already?" Mark railed back. "I came out because of you. I came out because

276

my friend had been kicked out of his house, and I was trying to get my parents to understand it. Just because I'm bi doesn't mean I have some magical closet I can leap in and out of as I please. There is literally nowhere else to go, and I don't care anymore. Yes, I am going home."

"And what about me?" Trevor said, tears in welling up in the corner of his eyes.

"You come with me, stupid. I assumed you knew that," Mark said with a hint of a smile.

Trevor walked slowly forward and put his arms around him. They held each other tight, along the side of the quiet road. Eventually they parted and started walking again.

"We need a ride." Trevor said, stating the obvious.

***

They sat against the dusty white brick of the little gas station facing a highway that no one but farmers used anymore. They were both pensive and guarded. After some debate, they decided that Mark would make the call. Without cell phones, neither one remember any of their friend's numbers. Calling Trevor's parents was a not much of an option, so Mark girded himself and asked the scabby clerk to use the phone and dialed his house. At each ring, Mark held his breath. He had no idea what to say when his parents answered. It wasn't like they were picking him up from the movies. He had been gone for almost three months.

When someone did finally pick up the phone, he almost hung it up. To his unexpected relief, Isaac greeted him.

"Isaac? It's Mark."

"Mark? Where the hell are you?" He could hear the excitement and relief in his brother's voice.

"I'm in Cache. We…need a ride." He didn't realize just how hard it was to force out those words.

"Everybody has been worried about you. We weren't sure where to look and…" Isaac talked a mile a minute before Mark had to stop him.

"Listen, I know. We just need a ride home."

"Is Trevor with you?"

"Yes. He will stay with us for a while."

"I don't know if… never mind… just tell me where you are, and I'll call Mom and Dad. We'll come and get you."

"Actually, I'm not sure I'm ready for them yet. Can just you come and get us?"

After a pause, "Yeah, I can get someone to drive me. I'll be there in an hour."

XXVIII.

The day continued to be clear and bright. The sun felt warm against the usual chill of the air. Mark looked up to see a familiar white Suburban coming their way. A thrill of panic shot through him as his parent's car turned towards them. As it pulled onto the gravel lot, the boys stood up. Before it had completely stopped, Isaac was already jumping out of the passenger's side. He rushed over to Mark and caught him in a massive bear hug.

"Christ almighty. You scared the shit out of all of us. Are you okay?" He didn't hide the emotion in his voice, and it brought tears to Mark's eyes.

"Yeah, I'm fine," was all he could manage. Until now, he hadn't realized just how much he had missed his brother. He had become too much of a realist to think that it would all be fine now, but in this moment, nothing felt better than to see family again.

They parted, and Isaac put a hand on Trevor's shoulder. "You okay, too?"

Trevor shrugged, but he couldn't keep the smile off his face. "Same as usual."

He wasn't, though. Neither of them were. Despite it all, even he felt relief to get back to civilization, regardless of the cost. He kept looking at the vehicle, expecting Mark's parents to come out. Mark also did the same but the only other person to emerge was his Aunt Caryn. She came rushing up and gave both boys a wonderful, smothering hug.

"I had to borrow your parent's car because I couldn't fit you all in mine," she explained. "I told them I was going to Costco."

"Thanks," Mark said. "Not just for coming to get us, but for lying."

"I understand." She took a good look at the two of them. "You two look like you've gone native." Their hair was long and scruffy, faces stubbly, and their clothes simply hung off of them. "You two have lost a lot of weight."

She tutted, herded them all to the car, and held back her tears of joy. A dark and mature air surrounded the boys, one that almost broke her heart. Their eyes didn't shine like before. No longer were these boys two wide-eyed teenagers but two souls who had done whatever it took to survive. She couldn't imagine what the two of them had gone through.

"Anywhere I need to stop before we get you home?" Caryn asked after they had all gotten inside.

"Oh my God! is there any way we can stop for a cheeseburger?" Mark blurted out. His stomach growled loudly at the idea of food. Trevor emphatically agreed with him.

"Two cheeseburgers coming up. When was the last time you ate?"

"Yesterday, I think." Trevor said, and Caryn's heart broke a little more.

Isaac started asking a million questions, but his aunt shushed him. She told him to wait until they had all gotten together and when Mark was ready. Mark appreciated that. He didn't mind answering his brother's questions, but not on an empty stomach. The rest of the car ride went by in silence, each person alone with their thoughts.

Mark had his head against the window. He watched the scenery speed past. It was nothing more than a blur of browns; the only difference lay in degrees. There was short scrub below puffs of scratchy sagebrush. Patches of dull green grass peeked out here and there. The ground rolled and pitched with the hills. Scabs of black rock pierced the ground, round petrified bubbles of stone dotted with dusty yellow and orange moss. The horizon was framed by snow-capped mountains.

He had lived here his entire life. This was his whole world, and still it held a desolate beauty. It was such a contrast to him. Grason was full of vibrant greens and tall trees and the colors of habitation. Farms surrounded the town like a vast protective barrier. But just outside of these, like a patient invader, lived the Idaho desert; the sagebrush and rattlesnakes always just on the outside.

The wind picked up as they crested another hill, the bumpy highway under them. What was it about this landscape, this desolate beauty that always made him so introspective, he wondered. He had so much space to think in. He squeezed his eyes shut. There had been too much thinking lately.

The back seat filled with trepidation as they pulled into the driveway of his house. Mark marveled at how nothing had changed but it looked so different. It seemed smaller, familiar but alien. The euphoria of the greasy hamburger in his stomach gradually faded as they walked up the front door. Caryn walked in first.

"I'm back," she called out.

LaVell stepped out of the kitchen and stopped dead as Mark and Trevor walked in.

"Thank you Jesus," he rushed over to his son.

Clara came hurrying from the back, babe in arms. She handed Rachel to her sister and went to her youngest son. As they embraced, Caryn doted on the baby and Isaac watched guardedly over the scene. He had been apprehensive about his parent's reaction. They had such mixed feelings about Mark running away that he wasn't sure if they would accept him with open arms or shun him. That they were so relieved to see him set him at ease. Once the emotions wore off, though, he wondered if they would still be so accepting. He couldn't fathom what his little brother had gone through. But this new, more adult version didn't seem like the type to let things go back to the way they were.

Trevor stood back behind everybody quietly watching the scene. He was truly glad that Mark was home safe and for his family's joyous reaction. Behind that sat a profound sadness. He knew there would be no such greeting for him at his own home. If he could even get in the door, that is. His father might not even let him get that far.

Caryn came up to Mark with baby Rachel. "You haven't met the newest Jensen! This is your sister, Rachel." The tiny cherub looked up at him with bright blue eyes. He gave her tummy a little tickle with his finger. She grabbed it with her chubby little hand. "I think she likes you." Caryn said with a smile. Looking down at her clear, innocent, face Mark began to get overwhelmed by a sudden surge of feelings. He hoped her future could be better than his present.

LaVell walked over to Trevor and put a strong hand on his shoulder. "It's good to see you too. I'm glad you're safe." Trevor read the man's face, and even if there was a shadow of blame for taking his son away, he knew that he meant what he said. "Your parents will want to know you are safe. You can call them."

"Um, no. That's okay. I'll just go over there and surprise them," Trevor said, already taking steps towards the door.

"No." Mark's voice stopped everyone in their tracks. "I know full well you aren't going home. We'll confront your parents together."

"Sweetie, he needs to let him them know he's safe. He has to go home." Clara said.

"He'll stay here tonight we can deal with them tomorrow." Mark said. It wasn't a question, and he wasn't asking permission. When neither of them protested, Trevor stepped away from the door.

"Are you hungry? You look like you've wasted away to nothing," Clara said.

"We stopped for burgers on the way," Caryn said.

Trevor and Mark exchanged glances, "Yeah. We could eat."

* * *

"It's been a long day." Mark yawned and stretched on the couch. After such an emotional day that had been topped off with a warm, home cooked meal and hot showers, he was ready for bed. A real bed.

"It's been a long couple of months," Trevor said, feeling just as tired as Mark did. He stood with Mark, and they both walked towards his bedroom.

As they passed, Clara said, "Trevor, I'll get you a sheet and quilt for the couch." The boys looked at each other and laughed.

"What's so funny?" she asked.

"We've been sleeping on the same moldy mattress for so long now, it's just natural of us to share a bed," Mark said.

"Well, that's not necessary now. That couch is perfectly comfortable. You've slept on it plenty of times." Undeterred she continued towards the linen closet.

"Mom, c'mon…" Mark started, but Trevor stopped him.

"It's no problem. I'm sure that couch will feel like heaven." He accepted the pile of linen from her. Mark watched him go then turned and gave his mom a hug. She stiffened and it didn't go unnoticed.

Once inside his old room, he stood there with the lights off. A sliver of moonlight peeked through the blinds. He stripped and stood in the moonlight, naked. He was warm and clean and fed for the first time in months. His ribs poked from his torso, so he counted them, then counted them again. Though so full of food, he wondered if the feeling of hunger would ever go away. Maybe he had lived with it too long.

Things were not the same as before, and he was not the same as before. He sensed a change in his parents too. Justified or not, his absence had caused this change. He felt responsible, and he didn't want to carry it. His mother seemed genuinely grateful for his return, but she wasn't comfortable around him. Mark wondered if had to do with what he did or what he was. Either way, it was better than what Trevor would be going into. He worried about what Trevor's parents would do. Would they even take him back? And if they did, would they accept him?

Tired and now getting chilly, he yawned again and slid into fresh sheets. They smelled wonderful and caressed his skin. The crisp smell of laundry wafted around him, but he missed the stale smoke smell he had gotten used to crawling into bed with. Deep-seated exhaustion had its way with him, and whatever worries he carried were to wait until tomorrow.

XXIX.

The boys slept late into the afternoon. Despite his homecoming, both of his parents still had to work, leaving Isaac home with them both. Caryn stopped by once but left when it became apparent the teenagers weren't going to wake up for anyone. At one point, Trevor awoke on the couch, blearily stood up, and stumbled into Mark's room to crawl into bed with him. Isaac did nothing to stop it; he only hoped they woke up before his parents came home.

When they finally did wake up, it was to a ravenous hunger. They ate their way through all the leftovers and then some by the time Clara and LaVell came home.

"We talked to your parents," Clara said as way of a greeting. "They will be here in a little while."

Trevor didn't say anything. He nodded and then stood to gather his stuff from Mark's room. Isaac took a fussing Rachel from his mother.

"And they are going to take him back?" he asked.

"Of course they are," she said and disappeared into the kitchen.

"Are we sure that's a good idea?" Mark asked his father. "I'm pretty sure they don't want him there." He tried not to sound vindictive.

"Aaron and Sandy are his parents, and he is a minor. It's where he belongs," LaVell said, but neither of his sons could find much conviction in the words. "Listen, we had a long talk with the two of them, and they agreed to let him back in the house. It might not be easy for him, but in a couple of years he can move out."

"If he lasts that long," Mark mumbled.

"Why can't he stay here?" Isaac asked.

"Because we're already at capacity," Clara called out from Rachel's room.

"I'm going back to school in the spring. He can have my room," Isaac suggested.

"We're going to finish converting your room into Rachel's nursery."

"He can crash in my room. We have the air mattress," Mark said and before she could build up the steam to reject the idea, Trevor cut her off.

"It's okay. I'll go wait for them outside." Trevor already stood at the front door. Mark could read his face. The feeling of abandonment was poorly disguised.

"I'll wait with you," Mark said, going for his coat.

"You're welcome here anytime." LaVell said to Trevor. He could feel the hot glare coming from his wife, so he said in a quiet voice, "If you need anything at all, let us know." The teenager responded with a nod.

In the late afternoon shadows, the teenagers sat on the front step and watched the occasional car drive by. "I'm sorry I took you from all this," Trevor said.

"You didn't take me from it. They didn't want me here," Mark pointed out. He knew that he and his family had a lot to talk about and some understandings needed to be established, but right now he was about his friend.

"Yeah, but they seem pretty happy you're here now. I have a feeling your parents are just forcing mine to take me back."

Mark didn't know how to respond to that, so he said nothing. The shadows gained more ground before a familiar Ford pulled up to the curb. Sandy Buell had one foot out of the car the moment it stopped. The boys stood, and before Trevor could move, Mark pulled him into a fierce embrace. When Mark let go, Trevor walked into his mother's arms.

"I'll talk to you tomorrow," Mark said, walking back into the house.

He looked back and saw Trevor's father still behind the wheel of the car. He refused to look anywhere but forward, his face an emotionless mask. Mark suddenly felt heart-heavy as he shut the door behind him.

"We need to have a long and serious talk after dinner," his father said from his chair

"Damn right we do," Mark agreed and went straight for his room.

"Don't think that just because we're glad you're home, it doesn't mean you're not in an incredible amount of trouble," he called after his son.

***

Later that night they ate at the dinner table as a complete family for the first time. It was a quiet and tense meal, most of the focus deflected towards Rachel, who seemed only affected by sitting still. Mark was grateful for the meal and being back in the trappings of home, but the tension hung heavily in the air. They all had so much to say, but none of them had the courage to start. More than once Mark attempted to say something only to lose nerve and compliment the dinner instead.

Isaac set his fork down with a clatter, finally unable to take any more. "I think maybe it's time to talk this whole thing out."

"You're right. We should," LaVell said. He put his fork down also. "Now that you're home, you realize I have to call the police."

"I guess I'm found now, huh?" Mark said.

"You're found. And you're also in trouble with the police. You might have to face a judge," his father continued.

"What? Really?"

"Yes. We had the police here and social workers who asked all sorts of uncomfortable questions. This isn't just a matter of you getting mad and deciding to punish us. It goes farther than that."

"I didn't run away to punish you."

"There are repercussions. To say that you are grounded would be putting it lightly."

"Why should I be grounded? It wasn't like I wanted to go. You didn't give me much choice." Mark's voice began to rise.

LaVell attempted to keep his voice level. "There is always a choice. Right Clara?"

"I have so many emotions. I don't know what to do with them all. I'm so happy and relieved that you are home safe but angry that you ran away and put us through all this," Clara said as she stared at the table.

"How can you be angry that I ran away? You didn't want me to be here in the first place," Mark said.

"What do you mean?" she stammered.

"Son, we would never want you to not be here," his father said.

"Really? On the night I left I listened to you after our argument at this very table. We had a fight because I told you I was gay. You both sat here and said that you weren't sure you wanted me around Rachel when she was born."

"We would never..."

"You did. I heard it. You said you 'didn't want this sort of thing around Rachel.' Your exact words."

"We were upset. It was a lot for you to drop on us," LaVell said. "We weren't ready for it. And it we didn't want to get rid of you. At the time, we wanted a way to make you the person we thought you were."

"I'm not that person. I had to pretend to be that person."

"So you still think you're gay?" Clara asked. Mark had a hard time telling if she was trying to be understanding or simply trying not to sound aggressive.

"Would it matter? Would it truly mater if I was gay or not?" he asked and felt his heart sink a little as he watched her wrestle with the question.

"We love you and just want the best for you, both for this world and the next. If you still think you're gay, then we love you anyway," she finally said.

"I don't 'think' I'm gay."

"We know it's not a choice. This is who you are," LaVell said. Judging by the look his mother gave her husband, she clearly didn't share the same thought. Mark appreciated his father's candor and felt like he might actually be on his side. But it wasn't the point he was trying to make.

"I don't think I'm gay because I'm not gay. I'm bisexual."

"What does that mean? You like both boys and girls?" his mother asked, confused.

"Yes, exactly."

"C'mon Mark. First you're gay and now this. Which is it? I don't know if this is some sort of rebellion thing or you really believe what you're saying," Clara finally exploded. "If you're gay, that's one thing. We can get you help. This...other thing... is just too much. You need to make a decision."

"Ever since I was little, I knew I liked guys," Mark began. "As I got older I started having the same feelings for girls too. It was hard for me to accept because I assumed that I was gay. I had gotten so used to the idea that I had to fight and hide homosexuality from you and this whole damned town. But with this, I just got more confused and had even less people to turn to. Like everyone else, I thought the world was black and white. It's not. It's more fluid than that. I had a lot of time to think about it, and it wasn't until I met my friend Anissa that I realized that I was just fooling myself thinking I wasn't anything more than what I was. And this is one part of who I am. Even Trevor has to come to terms with it, and he knows me better than you."

"The Book is black and white on the matter," his mother said with Sunday resolve.

Isaac, who had not made a sound the entire time, quietly spoke. "When we were kids, you and Dad told us that the Heavenly Father makes all the rainbows. Later, when I was a little older, we were talking about science and religion. I asked how a rainbow could be made from God if my science class said that a rainbow is just a spectrum. You told me He made the spectrum too.

"He made my brother just as he is. If he didn't like people who aren't straight, then He wouldn't have made him that way. This isn't some trial or test of faith. I don't see it as a punishment because nothing has been done to be punished about. To force him to hide who he is would make him a liar. I would be more worried about having a liar around my little sister than someone gay or bisexual."

Clara looked flustered, unsure of her feelings. She stood up and looked at her husband. "Do you feel the same way?" When he didn't answer immediately she murmured. "This is wrong. My little boy isn't some... I need to put Rachel to bed." She left the room. The men sat there facing each other.

Mark didn't have the proper words to express the immense gratitude he felt towards his brother at that moment, so he had to settle on the simplest way to say it. "Thank you."

"You're still a pain in the butt, little brother," Isaac said with a smile.

Their father stared at the table for a moment before saying, "When each of you was born, I kept my prayers to the Heavenly Father simple. I wanted nothing more than good health for you. For myself, I prayed a lot more. I wanted Him to help me guide you toward Him, and I wanted guidance in raising sons that were strong in character. Parenting is a rough road sometimes. As a parent, you get these perceptions of who you want your child to be. Even though you know they will go their own ways, you want it to be within a certain framework. When your child steps past that framework you built for them, it's hard to reconcile.

"I am blessed to have you two boys. Mark, I want you to know that your brother came down here from school and refused to go back until you were found. I am ashamed to say that he kept the faith longer and more diligently than your mother and I did. For that I am truly sorry." LaVell looked up at his youngest son for the first time during his speech. "I can only hope that your little sister grows to have the same virtue as her older brothers. I don't understand what you're going through. To be honest, I don't even really understand when you tell me you are bisexual. You are my son, and I know that you are a good person who has always followed what you believed to be right.

"I don't know what you went through these last couple of months, but I hope that someday you feel comfortable enough to tell me. Maybe I'll be strong enough to listen. Whatever happened, I know that you were watched over and that's why you came back home safe."

Mark blinked away tears. He stood and wrapped his arms around his father. When they separated, he asked, "What about Mom?"

"It's a lot for her to take. You'll just have to be patient and give her some time. She loves you. Always remember that."

"So am I still grounded?" Mark asked.

"Yes. That isn't changing." His father said and left the table.

XXX.

     The house seemed so much smaller and darker than Trevor remembered it. Walking in, he noticed that nothing had changed: the same almost threadbare furniture and same fading western art on the walls. But the walls were closer together, the ceiling a little lower, and the light didn't quite reach certain corners. He immediately put his things in his room. The air inside hung heavy and stale. He guessed his room hadn't been opened since he had left. If the house had gotten smaller, his room had shrunk twice that. He might as well be in a closet. The television in the living room came on, accompanied by the sound of dinner being prepared. Macaroni poured into water and pork chops slid into the oven. He took some comfort with these sounds. They were the sounds of the home he grew up in, but the familiarity chafed him all the same.

     The ride home slowed down time itself. His mother went on about how relieved they were that he was safe and how they worried about him. His father didn't say a word, didn't even look at him. Even now, he just sat in his chair watching television like Trevor wasn't there. Already restless, Trevor picked up his backpack and took it to the laundry room. He dumped the clothes in the washer and looked at them for a moment, detergent in hand. *Maybe I should just burn them,* he contemplated. He and Mark washed their clothes once a week in a bucket with a bar of soap. Everything was stretched out and faded. *I could burn them in effigy, but effigy to what?* He dumped the detergent in and aggressively turned the knob instead.

Dinner happened in front of the TV as usual. As they ate, Sandy asked her son generic questions. Where did he go? How did he eat? Did he make the right decisions when he had to? Trevor answered her question just as generically. Aaron still said nothing. Eyes glued to the set, he shoveled food in his mouth.

After dinner they continued to sit in the living room, watching the same police dramas that always dominated their evening. Sandy sat glassy-eyed on one end of the couch. She had taken her evening pill, apparently. Trevor decided to chance a question at his father.

"So, Dad, how's work been?" Trevor waited for a reply but only received a minimal shrug. He stood up. "I'm going to bed." Still no reaction.

Behind his bedroom door, he missed Mark. He hated the idea of sleeping alone, even on a real bed. When they were still in that cold and mouse-infested shack, he felt relief that he had gotten away from this house. But for a moment, as he got in the car to come home, he had a shimmer of hope that maybe he would to be welcomed back. He could see now that wasn't the case. He made a lateral move, from one hell to the next.

Sleep eventually found him in spotty bits and filled with staccato dreams. He woke up many times. At first he was too hot, overcome with a smothering feeling. Then he was cold from the covers being thrown to the floor. At one point he got up to get a drink of water.

Coming back from the kitchen, his thirst slaked, he heard his parent's bedroom door quietly open. Not in the mood to deal with them, he didn't say anything, just kept on to his bedroom. From around the corner came his father, nude and holding a revolver. The shock of it stopped Trevor in his tracks. When he heard the hammer of the gun cock, he found his voice.

"It's me, Trevor!"

"Thought you were someone breaking into the house," Aaron said, his voice thick with sleepy anger.

"Jesus. Next time try some underwear." Trevor turned away.

"I thought this is what you want, you like seeing this," Aaron said, finally lowering the gun. "Isn't this the sort of thing you ran away to find?"

"What the hell is wrong with you? This is not something I ever wanted to see." Trevor backed away. He heard his mom calling out unintelligibly from the bedroom.

"Watch your mouth. Get back to bed." Aaron turned and left his son to stand alone in the dark. Trevor heard his father say, "Well, I'm not used to that damned kid being back in the house."

"Is this real life?" he asked out loud to the dark.

***

Mark lay on the couch watching TV with his brother. The last couple of days since he had been home had been busy. They were able to get Isaac back in classes for the next semester, but only after a battery of phone calls and faxed forms. Christmas loomed

302

around the corner, so they all went down to buy a Christmas tree. He hadn't realized that the holidays were so close. It was a slightly surreal experience. Usually he grew excited by the idea of Christmas and buying the tree. To him it symbolized a warm and fuzzy season, a break from school, and a communion with Jesus. But as they brought their purchased pine into the house, the happy chatting came out staged and out of habit.

Later, over dinner, they had a debate about whether or not he should be homeschooled. This idea, of course, was brought up by his mother while everyone else shot it down. They all finally agreed they would talk with his principal.

Since being back in Grason, he hadn't left the house, and now the restlessness settled in. He had gotten used to walking miles just to get anywhere and had even looked forward to those walks. A lot of his time he spent going in and out of the little hovel he and Trevor had shared. A lot of time sitting outside until it got too cold and then sitting inside until he needed fresh air again.

Lounging on the couch became a luxury he enjoyed to the fullest, but now he needed to do something more than watch sports with his brother.

"Let's go do something. I don't even care what, just as long as I get out of this house." Mark yawned.

"I am under strict orders to make sure you don't go anywhere," Isaac said, his eyes not leaving the screen.

"C'mon. You'll be with me. It's not like I'm trying to make a break for it. I just want to do something. We can go over to the Rec Center and play some basketball."

"Sorry. We are not leaving the house."

Mark bristled but did so silently. He genuinely believed his brother worried about him, and to find out that he left school to look for his younger brother changed his perceptions of their relationship. The shadow he felt hovering over him all these years didn't belong to Isaac. He began to realize that he'd constructed himself.

"Hey, Isaac," Mark said. For a moment he struggled with the words. "Thank you for doing what you did. I know you left school for me, and I'm sure Mom and Dad had a fit about it. I just wanted to tell you I appreciate it."

"You're my brother. What else was I supposed to do?" Isaac gave him a shrug. With nothing else to say, they turned back to the television.

"Can I call Trevor?"

"Nope." Isaac said, again glued to the television.

"Is that also against the rules?"

"It is."

"Are you going to stop me?" Mark dared him.

His brother looked at him, "Nope."

Satisfied with his little victory, Mark disappeared into his room. He sat on the bed and dialed the number. When it rang, he was surprised to hear Sandy pick up. He had expected Trevor to be home alone.

"Hi Mrs. Buell. Is Trevor available?"

"Oh, hello Mark. He is, but he's not allowed to take any phone calls," she said politely.

"Is he grounded from the phone, or just not allowed to talk to me?" Mark snapped, then immediately regretted it.

"Well his father, you see…it's a complicated situation. I'm sorry," she said sympathetically. It wasn't complicated to Mark, but he didn't see the use in arguing with her.

"Is he doing okay?" he asked her.

"I'll talk to Aaron, and I'll see if he can call you in a few days," she said. He thanked her and hung up. He felt sure that Trevor's dad would prefer they never speak again.

Now he felt irritated as well as restless. He had gotten used to doing what he wanted, when he wanted, and that sort of freedom is habit-forming. He looked around his bedroom. The walls were adorned with posters and the surfaces with models and trophies. These things weren't his things. Not anymore. They belonged to a past version on himself. He stood in front of the wall of posters and tore them off the wall. One by one they came down. There was no anger in it. After his walls were clear he went to the shelves and bookcases, collecting the models of rockets and interplanetary landers. He gently tossed them into a pile on the floor.

Once he cleared everything, he came back with a garbage bag, stuffing it full of the discarded past. He dumped it in the trash can outside then lay back down on his bed and stared at the ceiling. It seemed all he was allowed to do.

In Cache he had formed the habit of losing track of time. Just to sit and let it slip past him, unnoticed. The habit took him again, and he fell into the fog of lost time. A knock at the front door surprised him out of it.

After a moment, Isaac poked his head in the room. "You have guests."

Mark bounded from the bed. Jennifer and Hannah stood by the front door. Jennifer came up to him and gave him a big hug. She lingered longer than he had anticipated. He wished it would have gone on longer. Hannah cocked an eyebrow and a half-smile. He wondered how much she knew. Though they had never been that close, she hugged him also, once Jennifer finally let him go.

"I'm glad you came back home. That place was…" Jennifer began but stopped as Mark's father walked in the house behind the girls. Mark hadn't even heard the car. Jennifer looked at LaVell then diplomatically finished with, "wherever you were wouldn't be good enough for you."

"It's good to be home, "Mark said. He believed his own words only to an extent.

"I heard you bumped into an old friend of mine," Hannah said. "How is she doing?"

307

"Eh. She's spending time in the closet, apparently," Mark said.

"I'm sorry, ladies. I'm sure you'd like to catch up with my son, but he's grounded," LaVell said. It wasn't harsh, but it was final. The girls looked at each other and Mark for an uncomfortable beat before saying hasty goodbyes.

"We never really did go over the terms of my grounding," Mark said after they left.

"I think we just did."

XXXI.

The next morning he woke from a familiar pounding on his door. "Get up, it's almost time for church," his father commanded.

Blearily, Mark did as he was told. He didn't mind. It gave him a chance to get out of the house. Showered and in his Sunday finery, he slid into the back seat of the Suburban.

"It will be nice to have you back at church, son," LaVell said as they pulled out of the driveway.

"Yes, it will," Clara agreed. "Behave yourself, though."

"What do you expect me to do, sit there and bring people over to the dark side?" Mark asked.

"Don't get snippy," she warned.

Isaac sniggered quietly and leaned over. "Luke," he said in a quiet "Darth Vader" voice, "come to the Dark Side and tell me 'who's your daddy.'" Both boys started laughing, much to their mother's annoyance, which made them laugh even more.

When they arrived, he was bombarded on two fronts. One, composed of folks welcoming him back and claiming they'd hoped for his safe return home.

309

Two, were those who pretended not to stare and kept their distance. The Buells' absence remained more conspicuous than if they had been there. Aunt Caryn stood by the doors, waiting for him. She took his hand, and they walked in together.

The service held nothing new for him. Just the usual litanies of Jesus' work for them or why he should work within each one. When the time arrived for the good people to rise and tell their tearful stories about their faith, Mark could feel his mom's eyes on him, urging him to do the same. He felt no need. He didn't want to give the congregation the satisfaction of a show.

"You should share your story and how it strengthened your faith," she whispered.

"Trust me, you don't want to hear what I have to say on it."

Through it all, he hadn't gained or lost any of his faith; it had simply changed. God wasn't the same benevolent father figure that he'd believed in before. The Almighty became a little more apathetic, he understood now. Humans were left to govern themselves, within a certain structure. They didn't need to compete for his love or prostrate themselves and beg for his acceptance. Gathering together in one building wasn't something He required. The Heavenly Father was love, and Jesus was sent to remind them of that important point. All the bickering, condemnation, and Sunday morning pageantry was so much rubbish. Sitting there at that moment, he understood that those moments in Cache, when felt so far from God, he was closer that he realized.

"People want to hear from you. They want to hear your story of faith and how it brought you home," she tried again. Mark recognized the edge of desperation in her voice. She needed to hear it, not the rest of the Ward.

"Mom, now is not the time."

"I have a testimony of faith." Clara sprang up from her seat. Mark groaned audibly, and his brother hid a laugh behind a cough. "My son was lost in the woods, almost literally. He became weak, and his faith was tested. In turn, his absence tested my family as well. In some ways it nearly tore us apart as our broken hearts yearned for our lost boy." She put a hand on his shoulder. Mark caught a glimpse of Isaac, who clearly wasn't impressed. For the first time, he wondered what really happened while he was gone.

311

"Through our Lord and Savior's love and grace, he came back to us. Every day, going forward, is just another testament to it." She hit her stride, and Mark could see folks nodding in agreement. His cheeks grew red. "Without Him we would all be like Mark, in the dark, confused, and scared. It's only His light that shows us the way out. That light brought him back home and one step away from that darkness."

"Mom," Mark said, unable to take it anymore.

"Mark's journey isn't over yet. It's with my family's renewed faith that we can help turn certain things out of His favor back around." A small tear slipped into the corner of her eye as she said it.

All it did was serve to turn his embarrassment to anger. He knew exactly what she was talking about. Looking up, he saw Jeordie Ward sitting across from him. Now that soccer was over, he had gotten chubby. He sat there watching Mark. The old rejection was nothing but a memory, but it still had a dull bite to it. It wasn't lost on Mark that Jeordie had made no attempt to talk to him. He had joined the town freaks now, a small but growing club.

"Or maybe it isn't a matter of faith but a matter of God making us *all* in his image," Mark heard himself say. The words were out of his mouth before he realized he had even said them.

The room became quiet, including his mother. Damp-eyed, she started to say something but stopped. The silence grew until Bishop Johns, standing at the front of the congregation, thanked her heartily for having the strength to share. Clara sat as he called for any other testimonies.

Time crawled as the tension between mother and son grew. Once the service was over, Mark couldn't get out of there fast enough. Flanked by Isaac and Caryn, Mark stood outside in the bright, chill air. Around them, people talked about Christmas plans and upcoming holiday programs. He knew that inside, where he couldn't hear, they were probably talking about him.

"So did it get that bad when I left? Did I cause so much grief?" Mark asked, knowing that his anger wasn't reserved solely for Clara. Some of it he put on himself and the pain he caused.

Caryn and Isaac exchanged a quick glance. "It was hard on us all. We all missed you very much and were worried sick about you," Caryn said. "Everyone dealt with it in their own way." Mark sensed a story here somewhere he wasn't being told. He made a mental note to ask Isaac about it later.

Soon his parents emerged, Rachel restless in her mother's arms. The three of them fell in step behind.

"We haven't had time to talk since you got back," Caryn said as they walked behind the others. "I wanted to give you some time with your parents."

"There has been a lot to go over" Mark said.

"How are things going? I've noticed your Mom hasn't called me since then. I think she's been mad at me since my little blowup at Trevor's parents while you were gone," she admitted.

"You got into it with the Buells'?" Mark was impressed. Trevor's dad scared the hell out of him.

"Your brother and I both did. We'll talk about it later," she said quietly.

Clara heard their murmuring. "You made an unnecessary scene. What that family does is their business," she said in a clipped tone while Rachel struggled in her coat and dress.

"I think it's a little bit our business since the boys ran off together," Caryn said. She made it sound as if they'd eloped instead of being kicked out of their homes.

"It was still embarrassing and needless. Trevor is back where he belongs, and Mark is back with us."

"When can I see Trevor, by the way?" Mark decided to weigh in.

"Be lucky we let you out of the house today," she said. "Here, take her." She handed the struggling baby to her husband. "Haven't you two spent enough time together? Maybe it's time for a break."

"Mom, you can't just…" Isaac started before Clara cut him off.

"I can and will. I'm still his mother and yours. I will do what is best for my family," she said, her voice rising.

"Honey, let's go," LaVell said.

"He's my best friend," Mark said. "You can't just keep us apart."

"You were out there with him doing God knows what. In fact, He does know, and that's why it was so important you came to church today," Clara said, building up steam for a tirade.

"It's not the Heavenly Father that has a problem. It's you." Caryn said, matching her sister's volume.

"You are going to stand here in front of the Lord's house and tell me this?" Clara yelled, unconcerned about appearance now.

"That's the point. The rest of us have reconciled it with the Almighty. Why can't you?" Caryn continued.

"So you think I'm a horrible person?' Clara asked acidly, turning her attention to Mark.

"No, Mom, I don't. I never did. But the truth is, you have to come to terms with it. This is who I am, and I'll be this way my entire life. I refuse to lie or hide it."

"So I'm not any better than the Buells', then?"

"Honey, not here." LaVell handed Rachel to Isaac then tried to guide his wife to the car, but she shrugged him off.

"I love all my children. I guess it's a sin to care now," she said as a parting shot then angrily got in the car.

LaVell rushed to the driver's side. The sooner he could get them out of there, the more he could contain the spectacle. Isaac stood by the car. He would rather stand with his brother than ride with his parents.

He looked at Mark, who shook his head. Reluctantly Isaac slid into the back seat.

Mark stood next to his aunt. He had no intention of getting in that car. Not right now. He'd go back home once she cooled off. The two of them stood there and watched the car drive off. The Mormon practice of seeing all but pretending to see nothing continued around them on the crisp December lawn. Neither of them seemed to care.

"Want to go get an ice cream while we give her some time?" Caryn asked.

"No. I'm tired of cold food, regardless of how delicious it is,"

"How about a beer then," she said, and he whipped his head around. "I'm kidding. Let's go back to my house. I'll make us some lunch." He nodded in agreement.

To his surprise Jeordie walked up to him. "Can we talk for a moment?" Mark agreed, cynically wondering where he got the courage to been seen in public with him. "I want to apologize to you," Jeordie said quietly. "When you left, it made me think of the way I handled things with us. I was unfair and scared. I had these feelings for you but… I don't know. They felt wrong, but they didn't at the same time."

"You pushed me away. It would have been one thing if you were just rejecting me, but you pretended to be something you weren't."

"I'm not proud of that. I could have handled it better. But I'm not that way. I'm not gay. I was hoping that we could still be friends."

Mark thought about it for a moment. "You had feelings for me?" Jeordie nodded. "You feel this way toward guys, but not girls?" Again a nod. "Tell me again how you're not gay?"

"I'm trying to do right by my family and by Him. I respect you for your decision to live so openly, but I'm not that brave. I need to get help to overcome this affliction."

"This 'affliction' is nothing more than living honestly. You'll be living a lie otherwise."

"I have to try," The corners of Jeordie's eyes welled with imminent tears.

"I can't support your decision, but somehow I can't hate you for it either. I'll see you when I get back in school." Mark walked away and rejoined his aunt.

"Please get me the hell out of here," he implored.

The air in the small car was thick as they both tried to dampen their raised feelings. Finally Caryn asked, "Planning on going back to school?"

"After the holiday break. Hey, can you take me by Trevor's house? I haven't even talked to him since we got back." When his aunt didn't answer right away he said, "Listen, I know that both my parents and his parents are probably trying to keep some distance between the two of us. I'm worried about him. I have this strange feeling that my parents did something to force them to take Trevor back. You know how scary his dad can be."

"I do. And I can't say I don't worry a little about him as well. They are his parents, though. I'm sorry, Mark, but your Mom is mad enough at me as it is."

"Yeah, sure. I'll try and call him when I get home. It just seems things are going better for me, sorta, but worse for him," Mark said, depressed.

"Mark, I need to apologize. I should have asked forgiveness the moment I picked you up in Cache, but the guilt weighed too heavily on me," Caryn said, the words exploding from her like a burst dam. "I feel a lot of this is my fault. You came to me for guidance, and all I did was betray your trust. I had no right to out you to your parents. I thought I was doing a good thing, talking sensibly to them and softening them up for you. Instead I put all this into motion, and I'm so sorry." Her eyes welled with impending tears.

"Aunt Caryn, I was angry at you for a while. But I don't blame you for it. The way my parents feel isn't your fault. And honestly, I don't think I could have lived the lie much longer. It felt like always wearing a coat that was too small and too thin. It gave no comfort and sometimes was so tight I couldn't breathe. But I had to wear it because it felt like the only protection I had.

"You tried to help, and I know you were on my side. Maybe I wouldn't have had to leave if you hadn't said something. Or maybe it would have caused something worse. Either way, you're still my favorite aunt," Mark said. They lapsed into a pleasant silence.

"Your mom will get over this, you know. Give her time," she said abruptly, trying to sound reassuring.

"That's what Dad says. I'd really like to think she will," Mark said, hoping it would happen soon.

XXXII.

The boys walked side by side to a lonely and brittle bench. The frosted grass crunched under their feet. They sat on the back, feet on the seat, and faced towards the meandering traffic of a mid-afternoon weekday. Mark set down the plastic bag he carried and pulled a Pepsi out. He opened it and took a drink, then passed it to Trevor.

"It feels like I haven't talked you in forever. After living together, days seem like weeks," Mark said. His breath was a plume on the air.

"And those weeks feel like years. Luckily Mom overmedicated this morning. She'll sleep most of the day. How much trouble will you get into if you're caught out of your cell block?" Trevor asked after taking a large gulp and following it up with a thunderous belch.

"I think Isaac will get into more trouble than I will. He's supposed to be watching me," Mark said taking the soda back. "My parents are both at work, and he was supposed to go to the store. He had a game on and sent me instead. I think he could tell I was getting antsy from being cooped up."

"Your brother is a good guy. I'd trade your entire family for mine right now. Everything seems rainbows and unicorn farts at your house."

"Eh." Mark shrugged. "It's still tense. Dad gets it. He accepts me for who I am, but I don't think he really understand why I left. Mom is still having problems with the idea that I'm not a straight Idaho Mormon boy. How is it with your parents?"

"Don't want to even talk about it." Trevor just shook his head. Being at home felt like a prison he could walk out of at any time. He had been instructed that under no uncertain terms was he to leave the house unless given permission. For once he listened to what he was told. He sat at home alone during the day most of the time but could walk out whenever he chose. His father had become scary, though. There had always been an overshadowing fear of him, only now it became more visible. He wasn't wanted, but he wasn't allowed to leave either. Everyday grew more maddening.

Most of his time whiled away in front of the TV, until his parents came home, then he went to his room and spent the rest of the time on the internet. No one had said anything about going back to school or church or anything else. He was just doing his time. He tried hard to not resent Mark for having an easier time back. It just made him miss Mark more.

He pulled two candy bars from his coat pocket.

"Hey, I thought you didn't have any money," Mark said as he took one.

"I don't." Trevor grinned and tore his open.

"Always the impulsive one. One of these days that's going to get you in serious trouble."

"I think we did pretty good, living with my impulsiveness," Trevor said with a mouth full of chocolate.

"Yeah, we did," Mark said.

They sat in a moment of shared experience. Their bond sang between them. To Mark, their recent time apart made the bond more tangible. Trevor feared that it might drive a wedge between them.

"So, did you tell your parents you were a fudge-packer or a switch-hitter?"

"Switch-hitter. I'm pretty sure they just see it as another flavor of gay, but they didn't try and kick me out for it. I'll take it as a small victory, I guess." Mark said. Trevor had nothing to say about it so they sat and chewed on their candy.

"I haven't seen any one of our so called friends since we got back. I feel so alone," Trevor said. "You seen anybody, or have they abandoned us both?"

"Yes. Jennifer and Hannah came by to say hi. Dad chased them off.

"So it's just me they've abandoned," he said glumly.

"I'm sure it's not that. They just haven't had the chance to come around yet," Mark tried lamely. He could feel a depression settle around Trevor. "Give it time. Remember, this is Grason. People don't associate with our kind in the daylight."

The corner of Trevor's mouth twitched. "Your girlfriend came to see you. How do you expect me to feel?

"She's not my girlfriend. We're not going to start this shit again, are we? I thought we had buried this whole bisexual thing already." Mark couldn't help feeling annoyed

"No. It's just…I'm a little jealous."

"Trevor, were we together? I mean, like a couple? Life in that hellhole was so chaotic and unconventional that it really didn't matter if we were a couple or not. We had each other and that's all that mattered. 'Boyfriend' wasn't a label that meant much. But now that we're back in the real world, is that what we were? Are we still?"

Trevor stood, "If you have to ask then I guess not."

"You know what I mean. We lived by our own rules. I want to know where we stand."

"So you can tell Jennifer if you're single or not?"

"Oh, Jeeze!" Mark yelled. "No. That has nothing to do with it. Honestly, I like her. Okay? But I am in no position mentally or emotionally for a relationship, with man or woman. What I do care about is you."

"You just said you weren't ready for a relationship, so it really doesn't matter."

Mark began to say something but stopped. He didn't have a reply. He didn't want a relationship, but he did want his friend to be happy. It didn't help that he still didn't know for sure how Trevor felt.

"Trevor, I…"

"I gotta go. My Dad will be home soon."
Trevor walked away, leaving Mark to stand there by
himself. Trevor turned once and yelled, "And for the
record, this isn't the real world. We were in the real
world, and apparently we couldn't hack it there either."
Mark watched Trevor as he disappeared down the
sidewalk before making his own way home.

***

Back in his room, Trevor dwelled on his
conversation with Mark. He knew his friend was right
about labels. Neither one of them had the luxury of
thinking like that. But Mark belonged to him. It didn't
matter if they were best friends, brothers, or lovers.
During that time, they had been all three.

Knowing Mark had been right felt just as bad as
if he hadn't been. Trevor sat alone in his bedroom,
alone in the house, and alone in the whole damned
town. Alone in the world. They may have loved each
other, but coming back changed things. Looking at his
cracked leather jacket hanging from a chair, it looked as
worn out as he felt. It had always symbolized freedom.
He put on that jacket and he lived beyond his parents,

school, church, and everyone else. Now when he looked at it, the only reminders left were of his taste of freedom. The taste that soured now. Every day he spent indoors, the walls closed in on him a little more. He contemplated leaving again. It would be easier, just walk out the door and never come back. But he had used up whatever luck he had. There was nowhere to go and no one to go to with.

He craved marijuana or even a cheap beer. Anything to take the edge off his existence. But there was no relief in sight. With both parents home for the night, he couldn't leave. Not that they would stop him. He doubted they would ever let him back in again if he did. He couldn't stay either. His depression was too heavy, but still he was restless. Outside of his door, he heard the murmurs of this parents talking. It skittered like insects scratching inside of his ears. He wanted them to shut up. He wanted them to be real people for once.

XXXIII.

Aaron Buell heard a sound in the kitchen. Instinctively he took the gun from the nightstand.

"It's just Trevor," his wife mumbled. Pulling on some boxers, he went to investigate nonetheless. Carefully he walked into the kitchen to see it was indeed just Trevor. The teenager sat at the kitchen table, a tall bottle in front of him. The only island of light came from the small bulb above the stove.

"Where did you get that liquor?" Aaron asked.

"Oh, don't act so surprised. I found it hidden in a cupboard, where you put it." He put a hand to his mouth in mock surprise. "Oh wait. Is it Mom's?"

"Don't you disrespect your mother."

"You want some?" he offered.

His father didn't say anything. so Trevor shrugged and took another drink. Aaron reached out and snatched it from his son's hand. He raised it up to slam it down on the table in anger but stopped. He slumped and took a seat across from his son. He placed the revolver on the table in front of him.

"I tried to do the right thing for you. We both did. But despite it all, you still turned out so…"

"Deviant?" Trevor offered.

"Maybe it's the Heavenly Father punishing us. Maybe it's a trial for us to overcome; I just wish I had the strength for it."

"So it's all about you. My entire existence is nothing more than God punishing you? Thanks."

"When you were born, I could tell you were a little off. Nothing showed, but I just sensed it. So desperately I wanted Sandy and me to have another one. It never happened. We were stuck with you. Now I'm being punished with a wife who can only function on pills and a son who's an aberration."

"So I never had a chance to begin with. The fact that I was born has been my greatest sin. I might as well go do a hundred guys then, for all the good it will do with you." Trevor reached for the bottle but Aaron slid it away. "I might as well just go jump off a bridge for all you ever cared."

"As if your soul hasn't collected enough degradation. You spit in the eye of your savior and this family if you kill yourself. There will be no kingdom of God for you. As if your queerness wasn't enough."

329

The disgust on his father's face would normally have made him flinch. Not anymore.

"It isn't about Him for you, and it never was. You can hide behind the Bible, Jesus, and the church all you want, but the real truth is I disgust *you*. You can't stand that your son never lived up to your ideals and that he went so far afield that you can't even stand to look at him!" Spittle flew from his lips as he railed against his father. Aaron just sat there, steely anger on his face. "I am who I am whether you like it or not. I know the only reason you took me back was because of the Jensens."

"They threatened to report your mother and me for child abandonment. I couldn't let those pretentious hypocrites do that to her. I really had no choice."

"Wow! Just wow! You know just how to make me feel like dog shit."

"If you don't want to be here, leave." Aaron said. They both recognized the empty threat.

"Don't you get it? It's not that I don't want to be home. It's that nothing has changed," Trevor said, close to tears. "I wanted to come back to a home, not this."

"You ran off."

"You kicked me out. I gave you a chance to find me, and you didn't." The charged air between them grew thick and tense. They didn't say anything for a moment. "Eli told me that he called you. You couldn't be bothered to care. You didn't give a shit."

"Watch your language. Yes, I knew where you were. And I also knew he would kick your freeloading rear out."

"To hell with you! I wish I had never come back here." Trevor stood up. "Maybe I'll just leave again."

"You stay right here. You'll go back to school, go back to church, and get your life straight," Aaron growled. "From now on, it's my way. Your life will be led by my examples and my word."

"Are you God now?"

"I am in this house."

"I'd rather be dead," Trevor hissed as they both looked at the gun.

"Don't be an idiot." Aaron said dismissively.

Father and son seethed at each other from across the table. Words were not needed to convey their feelings. They continued to stare at the gun that sat between them. Slowly, they looked up and locked gaze with each other, daring the other to blink first. Finally one of them did.

XXXIV.

Mark sat on the steps of the church. He had walked out halfway through the service. It was too much to take. His heart ached because of all the people inside talking about Trevor. So many whispers and accusations. None of them knew Trevor like he did, and he resented their tiny conspiracies. When he first got the news about what happened, he went numb. The lack of feelings, or what he felt should be appropriate feelings, still hadn't hit him. The thought of losing his best friend still didn't seem like a reality.

The heavy wooden door opened to a babble of hushed voices behind him. Many of them grew quieter as they noticed him. *Go ahead and talk it up*, Mark thought cynically. He no longer cared what any of them thought, but he wished they would shut up about things they refused to take the time to understand. None of them tried to understand Trevor, and they weren't making any attempts to understand Mark. When they asked if he was gay, he corrected them. More often than not, he received a glassy-eyed stare. Usually he turned and ended the conversation right there. The boldest asked if Trevor had been his boyfriend.

"I'm going to miss him," a voice said beside him. Jennifer joined him. The two of them sat in the middle of the steps, forcing the crowd to walk around.

"Me too," Mark said. "The dumb bastard left me behind."

"Hey, now." Jennifer looked at him. She didn't blame him for his grim attitude, but she hated to see it. "It's not like he asked for it."

"I know. Can't help being cynical, I guess." They sat there in silence. After a moment, a looming presence stood behind him. "I guess Mom is ready to go home?" Mark asked the presence.

"Yeah, she's getting snippy," Isaac said. Mark sighed and faced his brother. "You're not coming right home, are you?" Isaac knew the answer before he asked it. "I'll tell her." He walked off.

"You want some company?" Jennifer asked, standing with him.

"I appreciate it, but I'd better do it alone," Mark said. Jennifer gave him a hug and then let him go.

Mark hadn't gotten far before his mother's voice carried over the church lawn. Turning on his heel, he reluctantly heeded her call. He was in no mood to deal with her today. Isaac already had Rachel in the car. She fussed as he locked in the car seat. LaVell stood at the driver's side door pensively watching his wife and youngest son.

"Where are you going?" Clara asked.

"I think Mark could use a little time to himself," LaVell said. "I think he's entitled to it."

"I don't know…" she said.

"Hey, Mom, Rachel is getting fussy. Can you help me?" Isaac asked her. He nodded at his brother to take his chance to go. Clara went around to help with Rachel.

"Just be home before dinner," LaVell said. Without a word, Mark turned again and disappeared down the street.

Mark walked to his Aunt Caryn's house. Since the incident, he had come here often. He opened the front door and sitting there, sprawled across the couch, Trevor watched a faded comedy on television.

"I see you've made yourself at home already." Mark pushed him over and loosened his tie as he sat down.

Trevor grinned, a black eye turning from purple to yellow. "Where I lay my hat is my home. Isn't that how some old song goes?"

"You were the talk of church today. I had to duck out early. I couldn't deal with it."

"Can't handle my fame?" Trevor teased.

"Not that. They all talk like you're dead or something. Or like you're being sent to some internment camp instead of hiding out at my aunt's house."

"I know, and I really appreciate what your aunt has done for me. I can never go home, especially now that the restraining order has gone through. When my mom's cousin Gary comes down from Boise to get me, I'll be out of here for good. It's not like I'm ever coming back."

"Yeah." Mark turned away.

"Hey, don't worry about it. Once you're eighteen, you can come and visit me. Then maybe we'll head down to Austin and visit Anissa." Trevor's eternal optimism forced Mark to smile.

"Speaking of which, I talked to Fabiana yesterday. She and Ryan want to come to Grason and see you before you go."

"We can have another party. Hell, let's go back to Cache and really tie one on for old times' sake." Trevor had that gleam in his eye, the one that so often made Mark nervous.

"I really don't think that would be appropriate," Aunt Caryn said, walking in the front door. Trevor immediately sat up. "At ease," she said to him with a small grin. He slumped down again.

"I don't know how you can handle living with this slob," Mark joked.

"He's actually quite helpful. The dishes are always done and the trash is always taken out."

"Really?" Mark turned to Trevor. "You're clean and respectful for her? I lived with you for months, and you were a pig."

Trevor shrugged. "She feeds me." Mark rolled his eyes and shoved him.

Mark appreciated that she agreed to take him in, even if only temporarily. What even Trevor didn't know was that Mark and Caryn had discussed Trevor living there on a semi-permanent basis, just until they were both out of school. Caryn didn't completely discount the idea, but she didn't completely go with it either. Given his family's history, she strongly

337

suggested he put some distance between himself and his parents. Mark reluctantly agreed. Living on the other side of the state with some sympathetic family seemed like the best option right now.

"Just a heads up, I think your mom is getting suspicious," Caryn said to her nephew. She dolloped three bowls of pistachio pudding. "She stopped me before I could escape and started asking some loaded questions." It had been universally agreed that Clara wouldn't be told of Caryn harboring Trevor. LaVell had been the most adamant about it.

The three of them sat and enjoyed their bowls of post-church pudding. Once they were done, Caryn collected their dishes and took them to the kitchen. Mark knew he needed to go home soon, regardless of how much he didn't want to be there.

At the front door, they heard a couple of quick raps, and the door swung open. Clara took two steps in before anyone could react. She stopped in her tracks. "Trevor."

"Mrs. Jensen," he replied.

Caryn quickly rushed from the kitchen. "Now, Sis, I can explain."

"I hope so. The entire town has been looking for him." She looked at her son, shades of betrayal on her face.

"Not really, Mom," Mark said slowly. "Most of us have known the whole time."

"You just couldn't tell me, is that it?" Clara's face glowed red. "I'm only your mother. I'm just the one who took him in after you two decided to come back from hiding."

"Clara, listen, if you knew what happened..." Caryn tried.

"He needs to go back to his family. This is only encouraging these boys to run away as soon as things get rough. You'd think they would have learned their lesson by now."

"Hey, I'm not going anywhere." Mark stood up. "Why do you have to say it like that?"

"It's fine," Trevor calmed his friend. "There are reasons why I can't go home anymore."

"Well, there were rumors..." Clara said, deciding to at least hear him out.

"I'm sure there are tons of them. The truth is, my dad and I got into an argument late one night. He had a gun because he thought there was an intruder in the house. Instead, it was just me getting drunk in the kitchen." He ignored her reaction. "We kept going until we both got to a boiling point. He hated me, and he always had. In that moment, I finally realized it. Before that, I guess I had just told myself that he didn't understand me. Turns out he understood fine. He just hated me.

"We sat there, and maybe we both went a little crazy, or maybe we really wanted to kill each other, I don't know. We both reached for the gun, but he got it first. He pointed it at his only child. I looked in his eyes and hoped to see conflict. Instead I saw empty rage. For a split second I thought he would actually pull the trigger, and he might have. The fact is, for that split second, I wouldn't have minded, and that scared me the most.

"He lowered the gun and looked at it for a moment. Then he took each bullet out, one by one. He didn't look at me again. Standing, he left me alone in the kitchen. It took a second before I could breathe again. I got up and grabbed anything I could carry; I couldn't stay another minute in that house. I had almost made it to the front door when he came flying at me."

"'You aren't leaving unless I say you're leaving,' he snarled at me. 'You do what I say in this house!' He grabbed me. I swung at him, something I had never done before. That's when it turned into a fight. He kept screaming at me that I had to do what *he* said. That's where the black eye came from."

"What about your mother?" Clara asked. She still stood there by the door, her initial indignation draining away.

"She stood up for me for the first time that I can remember. I mean she really tried to protect me. Dad and I were wailing on each other when she came running out, yelling. Finally, she grabbed him and tried to drag him off of me. He pushed her away, and that's when I landed a good one on him. Mom got up and started slapping the crap out of him, yelling that she was going to call the cops on him. This time she was serious. She told me to go, to get out while I had the chance. So I did."

"What I can't understand is, if he doesn't want you, why did he make a big deal to keep you from leaving?" Mark asked.

"Because people like that see others as a matter of ownership and not as humans," Caryn answered him.

341

"It's about power. They need to feel they are in control no matter what. When they lose that sense of control, especially to something they don't understand, they become irrational," Clara said, looking at no one. "For some people, it's hard to see your children as individuals different as yourself. You just assume they are another version of you. Not everyone reacts well when they realize that they will be their own person and that person is so different." No one spoke for an excruciating moment. Sorrow spread across her face. She put it away but not before the others saw it.

"Sis, listen..." Caryn started.

"Mark, I'll see you at home. Take your time." Clara turned and walked out. As the door shut behind her, Mark stood up to follow her.

"Mom," he called after her as she walked down the sidewalk to her car. "Wait."

"Mark, I owe you an apology, one that seems too large for me to even know how to begin." She turned to him. "I was wrong, and I didn't want to admit it for so long. But with what happened to Trevor, I have to face what I've done too. I handled everything so wrong with you."

"This is what it took for you to realize? That's messed up," Mark said, but he had no anger in his voice.

"It is. I won't try and deny it. The worst part is, I realized it before all of this. I know you're not a bad person. It's just… I'd hear myself talk, and even my own thoughts. They weren't altogether right, but they weren't altogether wrong either. It was hard for me to reconcile the two, so I went the path of least resistance. What I had always known versus what I thought I had always known."

"So why did we have to go through all of this, then? Why did I have to leave and come back and then send my best friend away?"

"I can't give you any reasons, and I refuse to make excuses anymore. I am wrong, and I am sorry. I love you and always will. It's all so much for me to take, and I failed as parent when I refused to try and understand. Honestly, I don't know if I really get what you're going through, but that doesn't mean I can't be there for you anyway."

"It doesn't change what happened," Mark said.

"Mark. I'm trying here. This isn't easy. But no, it doesn't change what happened. It's hard for a

343

parent to admit they are wrong. Just know that I'm here for you now." She put a hand on his arm. He pulled away. But before she could react, he had his arms around her in a tight embrace. They stayed like that for a long time. When they parted, Mark continued to stand there as Clara got in the car. "I'll see you at home."

He watched her go then looked up at the pale winter sun. *Home is a subjective thing*, he decided. He was at home with Trevor in Cache and also with his parents in Grason. But not completely with either one.

"Home is where I don't have to hide anymore," He said aloud, taking a modicum of solace in the self-assurance that he would find his home eventually.

Resources for LGBT+ youth and beyond.

It's a rough world for everyone. More so for those who don't fit in gender and orientational norms. I've listed a few resources if you feel alone and need some help. While this list is geared toward youth in need, parents and adults who would like to some understanding can also check out these as well. If you are in crisis or in trouble, always try to reach out. If you feel there is no one to reach out to, keep the below in mind. Just know: *THERE IS ALWAYS SOMEONE TO REACH OUT TO!*

LGBT+ Youth Resources
Rainbowhealth.org
Advocatesforyouth.org
 Liveoutloud.info

Bi+
The BiCast.org – (podcasting for the bisexual+ communtiy)
BiNetUSA.org
Biresource.net

Asexuality.org - (Asexual Visibility and Education Network)
Interactoadovates.org – (Intersex youth)

Transgender
http://www.transyouthequality.org/
http://www.translifeline.org/
http://www.transstudent.org/

Runaway
www.1800runaway.org
nationalsafeplace.org
http://www.nrcdv.org/

Suicide / Crisis
http://www.thetrevorproject.org
http://www.suicidepreventionlifeline.org/
Text anonymous crisis counselor 741741

Acknowledgments

I'm one of those weird people that actually reads acknowledgments in books as if I might happen to know someone mentioned. I never do, but if nothing else, at least those folks get some sort of notice from someone. And yes, I will occasionally skim the credits of movies. Don't judge.

First and foremost I want to thank the scores of people that I know and grew up with in Idaho. You were a bigger influence on me than I had previously given credence to. Nicholas White (of 'Sly Lake Gang' fame) gave this thing its first beta test and with it the confidence that I might be on to something here. Melody Reeves, I thank you so much for dealing with me while I put it together and hammered on it, over and over again. Your patience and support will get you sainted one day. I'd also like to thank Lynnette McFadzen, of the Bicast, for not only giving it a more 'on topic' scrutiny, but also helping me with the resources. Last, but not least, G.S. Wright (of many and various books fame) for helping with all the publishing details that would have left me a babe in the woods otherwise.

Most of all I want to thank Sierra for inspiring me to write the book in the first place. If I can make the world just a little better for you, then that's all I can ask for.

About the Author

Michael R. Collins was born at a very young age in the wilds of southern Idaho. After a few decades he finally got his fill of all the sagebrush and rattlesnakes he could eat and journeyed forth to the creative bosom of Austin, Texas. Writing has always been tantamount to breathing, and he's done a lot of both. Harboring massive commitment issues, he tends to write across all genres. His previous novel, Night Shall Overtake, was published by Black Bed Sheet Books. He has also been published in Shadows & Light Anthology.

He plays bass, occasionally broadcasts his show Saint Zero's Headphone Bleed at szheadphonebleed.com, and is kind to animals and children.

Made in the USA
Middletown, DE
16 September 2021